Bob Shaw is th... ...ence
fiction nov... ...ide
reputatio... ...HE
PEACE M... ...TARS.
THE RAG... ...the British
Science Fictio... ...isted for the Hugo
Award; it was ... ...E WOODEN SPACE-
SHIPS and TH... ...VE WORLDS.

Born in Belfast, where he worked as a journalist for many years, Bob Shaw now lives in Warrington.

Also by Bob Shaw in Orbit Books

THE RAGGED ASTRONAUTS
THE WOODEN SPACESHIPS
THE FUGITIVE WORLDS

BOB SHAW

Dark Night in Toyland

ORBIT

An Orbit Book

First published in Great Britain in 1989 by
Victor Gollancz Ltd
This edition published in 1991 by
Orbit Books, a Division of
Macdonald & Co (Publishers) Ltd
London & Sydney

"Dark Night in Toyland" was first published in *Interzone*, 1988.
"Go On, Pick a Universe" was first published in *The Magazine of Fantasy & Science Fiction*, 1981.
"Stormseeker" was first published in *Galaxy*, 1972.
"Aliens Aren't Human" was first published in *Extro Science Fiction*, 1982.
"Love Me Tender" was first published in *New Terrors*, 1980.
"To the Letter" was first published in *Interzone*, 1989.
"Cutting Down" was first published in *Isaac Asimov's Science Fiction Magazine*, 1982.
"Hue and Cry" was first published in *Amazing*, 1969.
"Dissolute Diplomat" was first published in *IF*, 1960.
"Well-Wisher" was first published in *The Magazine of Fantasy & Science Fiction*, 1979.
"Executioner's Moon" was first published in *Imagine*, 1985.
"Deflation 2001" was first published in *Amazing*, 1972.
"Shadows of Wings" was first published in *More Magic*, 1984.

Printed in Great Britain by
BPCC Hazell Books
Aylesbury, Bucks, England
Member of BPCC Ltd.

ISBN 0 7088 8342 7

Orbit Books
A Division of
Macdonald & Co (Publishers) Ltd
Orbit House
1 New Fetter Lane
London EC4A 1AR
A member of Maxwell Macmillan Pergamon Publishing Corporation

To Arthur C. Clarke

CONTENTS

CONTENTS

INTRODUCTION

"Daddy, why are my fingernails made of plastic?"

The question came from my youngest daughter, then aged about four, who had just examined her hands, almost as though seeing them for the first time. I looked at her fingers and saw that the nails were indeed little translucent slivers, not much different in appearance from that shiny pink plastic which is used in making tiny dolls. *I* knew the true situation, but the child had accepted that she was a composite being – part flesh, part Woolworths plastic – and I suddenly saw a little way into the gulf that existed between her universe and mine.

The little episode gave me a cold feeling in the stomach, one which was accompanied by that turmoil at the centre of the being which authors sometimes describe as inspiration. And within a minute I had the idea and plot for DARK NIGHT IN TOYLAND, the lead story in this collection. You might describe it as science fiction, fantasy or horror – depending on your academic stance in these matters. I would hesitate to classify it, but would say there is something uniquely horrible in the idea that there might be no clear dividing line between the sacred body of one's own child and the increasingly clever, increasingly complex products of the commercial toy manufacturer.

The above will, I hope, show why it is that when writers are confronted by that perennial question – where do you get your ideas from? – their eyes often cloud over and the muscles around their mouths become visibly agitated, but without any audible consequence. The workings of the creative mind cannot be explained. A skilled writer can deliberately manufacture a story he *knows* will sell in its intended market; or he can be struck by an inspirational bolt from the unknown and decide to take his chances on the resultant story ever finding an audience.

One of the pleasures of working in the science fiction and fantasy field is that the short story form is still very much alive there, and also that – literally – anything goes. Rules do exist, but they are not imposed on the writer from outside or above. A story can be an extended joke, an attempt to reach the dim boundaries of the imagination, a puzzle in disguise, a bad dream excised from the subconscious by the scalpel of language, or a personal statement about the perplexities inherent in being part of the human race.

All of the stories in this collection fall into one or more of the above categories – but which into which? No matter to which category you assign a particular piece I could argue for hours that others would have been more appropriate – especially if there was a little whisky available to lubricate the gearwheels of discussion. The most important thing, however, is that you should find at least some of these varied offerings enjoyable.

I hope you do!

DARK NIGHT IN TOYLAND

"Don't let it happen today," Kirkham prayed.

And then that other side of him, that intruder whose caustic, sneering voice had been growing more and more insistent for the past month, cut in with: *Yeah, it's bad enough for a kid to die of cancer at any time – but if it happens on Christmas Day it makes him feel rotten.*

Kirkham jumped to his feet and strode violently about the study, ashamed and afraid of the voice even though he was sufficiently Manichaean in outlook to understand why he heard it. The oak-panelled room had once seemed so right for a small-town Methodist minister whose mission was the preservation of religious belief in the hostile climate of the 21st century. Now it seemed dark and claustrophobic. He went to the window and pulled aside the green velvet drapes. It was ocean-black outside – six o'clock on a Christmas morning. No different to six o'clock on any other morning in winter.

The voice again: *Here it is, Christmas – and us out here chasing a star.*

Kirkham gnawed the back of his hand and went into the kitchen to brew coffee. Dora was there in her powder-blue dressing gown, making herself busy with cups and spoons. Straight-backed. Brave woman, their friends and neighbours must have been saying, but only Kirkham knew the extent to which she had been defeated by Timmy's illness.

One night when he had talked to her about faith she had said, with a kind of sad contempt, "Do you have faith that two and two make four? Of course not, John. Because you *know* two and two make four." It had been the first and only time she had spoken to him in that manner, but he had a disturbing conviction she had been making a personal statement about life and death.

"I didn't hear you come down," he said. "Isn't it a little early for you?"

Dora shook her head. "I want this day to be as long as possible."

"It won't work, Dora." He knew at once what she was trying to do. Dostoyevsky on the morning he was led out to be executed, resolving to magnify and subdivide every second so as to expand an hour into a lifetime.

"You have to let time go," he said. "With gladness. It's the only way to tackle eternity." He waited, aware he had sounded pompous, hoping she would challenge him and thus admit her need for his help. And thus establish, in his own mind, that he was able to help.

"Milk or cream?" she said.

"Milk." They sipped their coffees for a moment, separate, the bright clean geometries of the kitchen shimmering between them.

"What are we going to do next Christmas, John?" Dora's voice was matter-of-fact, as though discussing arrangements for a vacation. "When we're alone."

"We have to see what God has in store for us. Perhaps, by then, we'll understand."

"Perhaps we understand already. Perhaps the only thing we have to understand is that there is nothing for us to understand."

"Dora!" Kirkham felt a sombre excitement over the fact that his wife seemed on the brink of acknowledging her disbelief. He knew he would be unable to help her unless it was brought out into the open. The words had to be said, the thoughts translated into mouth movements and air vibrations, even though the eyes of God could see everywhere.

The voice: *Great eyesight, God has. I mean, how else could he sit at the centre of the galaxy and fire a cosmic ray across thousands of light years and hit a single cell in a little boy's spine? That's real sharpshooting in anybody's book. Especially the Good Book . . .*

Kirkham's attention on Dora's face wavered. Of all places, it had had to be the spine, where the living structures were too complex for successful reproduction by bioclay. The treatment had been applied, of course, using the most advanced compounds, and it had given Timmy a few extra months. For a time it had even seemed that a cure might be achieved (the breakthrough had to come someday) but then the boy had begun to lose the mobility of his left leg – first signs that the bioclay, which was displacing cancer cells as quickly as they were formed, was proving unequal to the task of recreating the original tissues.

" . . . be awake by this time," Dora was saying. "Let's go in."

Feeling that he had missed an important opportunity, Kirkham nodded and they went into Timmy's room. In the dim glow of the nightlight they could see that the boy was awake, but he had not touched the Christmas gifts which were stacked at his bedside. Kirkham learned, yet again, how the word heartbreak had originated. He hung back, afraid to trust his voice, while Dora went to the bed and kneeled beside it.

"It's Christmas morning," she coaxed. "Look at all the presents you have."

Timmy's eyes were steady on her face. "I know, Mum."

"Don't you want to open them?"

"Not now – I'm tired."

"Didn't you sleep well?"

"It's not that sort of tiredness." Timmy looked away from his mother, his small face dignified and lonely. Dora lowered her head.

He knows, Kirkham thought, and was galvanised into action. He hurried across the room and began opening the varicoloured packages.

"Look at this," he said cheerfully. "From Uncle Leo – an audiograph! Look at the way it turns my voice into colour patterns! And here's a self-moving chess set . . ." He went on opening parcels until the bed was covered with gifts and discarded wrappings.

"This is great, Dad." Timmy smiled. "I'll play with them later."

"All right, son." Kirkham decided to make one more attempt. "Isn't there anything you specially wanted?"

The boy glanced at his mother, suddenly alert, and Kirkham felt grateful. "There was one thing," Timmy said.

"What is it?"

"I told Mum last week, but I didn't think you'd let me have it."

Kirkham was hurt. "Why shouldn't . . . ?"

"It's a Biodoh kit," Dora put in. "Timmy knows how you feel about that stuff."

"Oh! Well, you must admit it's not . . ."

"But I bought it for him anyway."

Kirkham began to protest, then he saw that – despite the encumbrance of paralysed legs – Timmy was struggling into an upright position in the bed, face filled with eagerness, and he knew it would be wrong to interfere at that moment. Dora went to a closet and brought a large flat box which had not been gift wrapped. Printed across it in capacitor inks which made the letters flash regularly, like neon signs, was the word "BIODOH". Kirkham felt a stirring of revulsion.

"Is it all right, Dad? Can I have it? You won't be sorry." Timmy was almost out of bed. His pyjama jacket had crumpled up, exposing the edge of the therapeutic plastron the surgeons had attached to his back.

Kirkham made himself smile. "Of course, it's all right."

"Thanks, John." Dora's eyes signalled her gratitude as she made Timmy comfortable against his pillows and moved the other presents to a table.

Kirkham nodded. He went to a window, drew back the curtains and looked out. The panes were still enamelled with night's blackness, reflecting the scene within the bedroom. A child in a warmly lit cot, his mother kneeling by his side. The associations with the first Christmas, which might have comforted Kirkham earlier, seemed blasphemous in the presence of Dora's gift. He wanted to leave the room, to find peace to think, but there was a risk of spoiling his son's unexpected happiness. He returned to the bedside and watched Timmy explore the compartments and trays of the Biodoh box.

There was the pink dough which represented surface flesh; reddish slivers which would serve as muscles; coiled blue and yellow strands for nerves; plastic celery stalks for major bones; interlocking white beads for vertebrae. Small eyes arranged in neat watchful pairs. Snap-on nylon hooks for muscle inserts, the silver plugs of nerve connectors. And – most hideous of all to Kirkham's eyes – the grey putty, debased commercial relative of the bioclay which was at work in Timmy's spine, which could be fashioned into ganglia. Primitive little brains. The boy's fingers fluttered over the box, briefly alighting on one treasure and then another.

Kirkham looked at the discarded lid on the floor. "BIODOH helps your child understand the Miracle of Life!" *The fools*, he thought, *don't they know that if you understand a miracle it ceases to be a miracle?*

Timmy leafed through the glossy instruction manual. "What should I make first, Mum?"

"What does it suggest?"

"Let me see . . . a giant caterpillar! Simple invertebrate . . . blind . . . Shall I try it? Right now?"

"There's no time like the present," Dora said. "Come on – I'll help."

They put their heads together and – working intently, with frequent consultations of the manual – began to build an eight-inch caterpillar. A muscle strip of suitable length was chosen first. Load-spreaders, like miniature umbrellas, were attached to each extremity. A blue nerve cord was added, cut in two at the centre of its length and silver nerve connectors fitted to the severed ends.

Pale green surface flesh was taken from the appropriate compartment and formed in the shape of a hotdog roll which had a longitudinal slit. The muscle, complete with nerve, was then laid in the slit and the load-spreaders were firmly pressed into the green flesh at each end.

Finally, Timmy took a pellet of the grey putty, pressed it against his wrist and determinedly opened and shut his hand in a steady rhythm for about a minute, to imprint the nerve impulse pattern in the receptive material.

"This is it," he said breathlessly. "Do you think it will work, Mum?"

"I think so. You did everything exactly right."

Timmy looked up at his father, seeking praise, but Kirkham could only stare at the lifeless green object on the workboard. It both horrified and fascinated him. Timmy dropped the grey pellet into the thing's interior and pressed the two silver nerve connectors into it.

On the instant, the caterpillar began to squirm.

Timmy gave a startled cry and dropped it. The pseudo-creature lay on the board, sideways, stretching and contracting. At each contraction its body opened obscenely and Kirkham saw the muscle swelling within.

You lied to us, Christ, he thought in his dread. *There is nothing special or sacred about life. Anybody can create it – therefore we have no souls.*

Timmy laughed delightedly. He picked up the caterpillar and sealed it along its length by pressing the sides of the wound together. The pale flesh melded. Timmy, working with uncanny certitude, fashioned little foot-like blobs along the creature's underside and set it down again. This time, stabilised and aided by its feet, the caterpillar crawled along the workboard, moving blindly, with the rhythm it had learned from the boy's clenching fist. Timmy looked into his mother's face, triumphant, intoxicated.

"Good *boy*!" Dora exclaimed.

Timmy turned to his father. "Dad?"

"I . . . I've never . . ." Kirkham sought inspiration. "What name are you going to give it, son?"

"Name?" Timmy looked surprised. "I'm not going to *keep* it, Dad. I'll need the materials for other projects."

Kirkham's lips were numb. "What are you going to do with it?"

"Put it back into inventory, of course." Timmy lifted the dumbly working caterpillar, split it open in the middle with his thumbs and extracted the grey pellet. As soon as the nerve connectors were separated from the ganglion the pseudo-creature lapsed into stillness.

"That's all there is to it," Timmy commented.

Kirkham nodded, and left the room.

*

"I'm sorry to have to say this, John and Dora, but your boy has very little time left." Bert Rowntree stirred the tea Dora had made for him, his spoon creating irrelevant little ringing sounds in the quietness of the afternoon. His brow was creased with unprofessional sadness.

In contrast, Dora's face was carefully relaxed. "How much time?"

"Probably less than a week. I've just taken new tissue compatibility readings, and the ratio is falling off very quickly. I . . . There's no point in my trying to paint a falsely optimistic picture."

"We wouldn't want you to do that, Bert," Kirkham said. "You're sure there'll be no pain?"

"Positive – the bioclay has built-in blocks. Timmy will simply go to sleep."

"That's something we can thank God for."

Dora's hand quivered abruptly, causing a rivulet of tea to slip down the side of her cup, and Kirkham knew she had wanted to challenge him. *You mean, something we can thank the makers of bioclay for.* He wished again that she would voice her thoughts and begin the process of spiritual catharsis. She had to be reassured that God's message had not changed and never would change.

Come off it, John, that other Kirkham snickered, *you don't take everything in the Bible as gospel.*

"Timmy was showing me his Biodoh kit," Rowntree said. "He seems to have made some quite advanced constructions."

"He has a talent for it." Dora was calm again. "He got on so well I had to buy him all the supplementary packs. Equilibrium units, voice simulators – that sort of thing."

"Really?"

"Yes, though I haven't seen everything he's been doing. He says he's going to give me a special surprise."

"It's incredible that he's been able to go so far in such a short time."

"He has the touch. It's a pity that . . ." Dora stopped speaking and shook her head, choking up.

"I don't think I like him having that stuff," Kirkham said. "There's something unwholesome about it and I think it takes too much out of him."

"Nonsense, John. If you want my professional opinion, you were very lucky to find something to occupy the boy's mind at this stage. Keeps him from brooding too much."

"That's the way I feel about it," Dora said, scoring a point over Kirkham.

Rowntree finished his tea and set the cup down. "You have to admit that Biodoh is a fascinating material. You know it's an unrefined form of surgical bioclay? Well, I've read the impurities in it sometimes introduce random properties which lead to some very strange effects. In a way, it suggests that life itself is . . ."

"If you don't mind," Kirkham interrupted, getting to his feet, "I have to record this week's sermon."

Rowntree stood up too. "Of course, John – I'm due back at the clinic anyway."

Kirkham saw the doctor to the door and when he returned he found that Dora had gone upstairs, probably to Timmy's room. He hesitated for a moment, then went into his study and tried to work on his sermon, but suitable words refused to assemble in his mind. He knew what Rowntree had been about to say, and the other Kirkham kept repeating the same statement.

Life itself, the relentless voice gloated, *is only a chemical impurity*.

On the eighth day of January Timmy drifted into a coma, and from then on John Kirkham and Dora could do nothing but wait. The prolonged vigil had a dreamlike quality for Kirkham because he felt it was outside of normal time. His son had already left one world and was awaiting the completion of certain formalities before he could be admitted to the next.

Now that the ultimate trial had begun, Kirkham found himself enduring better than he had feared. He slept quite a lot, always for short periods, and occasionally awoke with the conviction that he had heard sounds of movement from Timmy's room. But each time he opened the door and looked in, the boy was lying perfectly still. Pea-sized lights on the diagnostic panel at the head of the bed glowed steadily, in fixed patterns, indicating that there had been no abrupt changes in Timmy's condition.

The only hint of activity came from the light-pulsing inks on the lids of the Biodoh boxes which, at Dora's insistence, were stacked by the bed. Their presence was still an affront to Kirkham, but during the night hours – while Dora and Timmy slept – he had confronted and overcome his fears.

The reason he abhorred Biodoh was that it appeared to give men, women, *children* the ability to create life. That led logically and inescapably to the annihilation of God, which in turn meant that the personality known as Timmy Kirkham was about to be snuffed out of existence for ever. Only God – not the manufacturers of Biodoh kits – could promise life beyond the grave.

Kirkham had found a simple, if distasteful, solution to his problem.

His own giant caterpillar had not been nearly as good as Timmy's first effort, and that had made the task of dismantling less harrowing than he had expected. The silver plugs came easily out of the grey module and all movement ceased. A purely mechanical operation. Nothing to get upset about.

His second project was a slightly larger caterpillar, with a single eye, which would crawl towards a source of light until the intensity of radiation passing through the iris reached a certain level, at which point the pseudo-creature would turn away. That, too, had been far less successful than Timmy's version – Dora had been right when she said the boy had a special talent – but it had crawled towards the light, hesitated, turned away, wandered, and then had been drawn to the brightness again in a manner which suggested complex motivations.

Kirkham's understanding of its operating principles, however, had enabled him to see that it was no different to a battery-powered toy car which would not run over the edge of a table. He realised, with a surge of gladness, how naïve he had been to equate a crude Biodoh construction with the unique complexity of a living being.

And, in the throbbing quietness of that night-time hour, while his son slipped nearer to death, it had been an emotionally neutral experience for Kirkham to scoop up the one-eyed caterpillar, open its belly, and return its various components to inventory.

Timmy died on the twelfth day of January, in the early hours of the morning.

John and Dora Kirkham stood beside the bed, hand in hand, and watched the lights on the dianostic panel gently extinguish themselves. Mercifully, there was no other sign of the final event taking place. Timmy's small face shone with the peaceful lustre of a pearl. Kirkham could feel other lights fading away within himself – God had never intended the loss of a child to be entirely reconcilable – but one precious flame continued to burn steadily, sustaining him.

Dora gave a deep, quavering sigh and grew heavy in his arms. Kirkham led her from the room and into their own bedroom. Accepting his guidance, she lay down on the divan and allowed him to draw the duvet over her.

"I want you to stay here for a while," he said. "Try to get some rest. I'm going to call the clinic." He went to the door.

"John!" Dora's voice was weary, but firm.

"What is it?"

"I . . . I've been making things harder for you – but I was wrong. I was so wrong."

"I know you were, darling. As long as you realise it, nothing else matters."

She managed something like a smile. "It happened just as Timmy was leaving us. I just *knew* it couldn't be the end. I knew we would see him again."

Kirkham nodded, fulfilled. "You've got the message. Don't lose sight of it. Not ever!"

He turned out the light, closed the door and went towards the stair. From his right there came a scrappy little sound, like that of a small object falling over. He halted in the middle of a stride. The sound seemed to have come from Timmy's place of rest.

Without giving himself time to think, Kirkham flung open the door of his son's bedroom. Timmy's body lay calm and unmoving in the dim light. Not knowing what he had expected, Kirkham advanced into the room.

I should have covered his face, he thought.

He approached the bed and drew the sheet upwards over the carved marble features. An instinct prompted him to pause and brush strands of hair away from the child's dewy forehead. He had completed covering the body when he became aware of several crumbs of grey material clinging to his fingers. It looked like Biodoh cortical putty.

It can't be, Kirkham told himself. *You're only supposed to press it against your wrist. Timmy can't have been pressing it against his forehead – that's not in the instruction manual.*

There was a sound from behind him.

Kirkham whirled, his hands fluttering to his mouth as he saw the tiny upright figure emerge from the shadows of a corner. It walked towards him, arms outstretched, dragging its left leg as Timmy had once done. Its lips moved, and Kirkham thought he heard a faint distorted sound.

Da . . . Da . . . Dad.

He threw himself backwards and fell, overturning a chair. The figure came closer – naked and pink, moving with a ghastly crippled clumsiness – while he lay on the floor and watched. Its lips continued to move, and its eyes were fixed on him.

"John?" Dora's voice filtered out of another universe. "What's the matter, John?"

Kirkham tried to visualise what would happen if Dora came into the room – suddenly he was competent, able to protect her from the fate which had already overtaken him.

"There's nothing wrong," he called out. "Stay where you are."

He rose on to his knees and allowed the miniature figure to approach him. *Suffer little children to come unto me*, his other self quoted, sneering. Kirkham closed his eyes and waited till the smooth cool body blundered against his legs. He lifted it, and, using his thumbs, split it open at the thorax, exposing the nerve cords running up into the head. He hooked a fingernail around

them and pulled them out, and the small object in his hands
ceased to move.

All I have to do is return the parts to inventory, he thought,
keeping his gaze averted from the figure in the bed, smiling his
new kind of smile.

A purely mechanical operation . . .

GO ON, PICK A UNIVERSE!

The shop, which was about a hundred yards off Fifth Avenue, was so discreet as to be almost invisible. Its single front window was blanked by heavy drapes, and down in one corner it bore small bronze letters which said ALTEREALITIES INC. The peach-coloured light from within was so subdued that, even in the gathering darkness of a December afternoon, it was difficult to be sure the place was open for business.

Arthur Bryant hesitated for a moment on the sidewalk, trying to overcome his nervousness, then opened the door and went in.

"Good afternoon, sir – may I help you?" The speaker was a swarthy young man with slaty jowls and a dark business suit that had an expensive silkiness to it. He was seated at a large desk on which was a nameplate proclaiming him to be one T. D. Marzian, Branch Manager.

"Ah . . . I'd like some information," Bryant said, taking in his surroundings with some interest. A plump girl with cropped brown hair was seated nearby at a smaller desk. The ambience was one of deep carpet, hessian walls and intimate whispers of music. The only item which distinguished the place from a thousand other plushy front offices was a silvery disk about the size of a manhole cover which occupied an area of carpet behind the two desks.

"Glad to be of service," Marzian said. "What would you like to know?"

Bryant cleared his throat. "Can you really transfer people into other universes? Universes where things are different?"

"We do it all the time – that's our business." Marzian's jowls parted to make room for an easy, reassuring smile. "All a client has to do is specify his ideal conditions, and – provided they are not *so* preposterous that they can't exist anywhere in the multitude of alternate realities – we relocate him in the universe of his dreams. Our Probability Redistributor operates instantaneously, painlessly and with total reliability."

"It sounds marvellous," Bryant breathed.

Marzian nodded. "It *is* marvellous – well worth every cent of the fee. What sort of reality parameters did you have in mind?"

Bryant glanced in the direction of the plump girl, turned his back to her and lowered his voice. "Do you think . . .? Would it be possible . . .?"

"There's no need to be embarrassed, sir – we have a lot of experience in meeting customers' various personal requirements, and our service is absolutely confidential."

"I was wondering," Bryant mumbled, "if you could transfer me to a reality in which . . . er . . . I had the most perfectly developed physique in the world?" His diffidence was caused by the fact that he was five-four in his shoes and had no other dimensions that he cared to discuss. He waited, enduring the other man's scrutiny, half-expecting a look of derision – but Marzian appeared to be in no way amused or perturbed.

"We most certainly could – no problem whatsoever." Marzian spoke with breezy confidence. "You know, for a moment you almost had me convinced you were going to ask for something difficult."

Bryant experienced a pang of purest joy. Until that moment he had not really dared believe that his dream could be fulfilled anywhere in the multiple-probability universes, but now he could begin planning the sort of life he would enjoy as an adulated superman. *I'll have five different women every day for a month*, he thought, *just to break the new body in. Then I'll settle down to a life of moderation – maybe only two or three women a day . . .*

"There is just the matter of the fee," Marzian was saying. "A hundred thousand dollars may seem a lot, but the cost of installing and running the Probability Redistributor is astronomical – and the fee does cover our unique Triple Chance facility. What it amounts to is that, if necessary, you get up to three transfers for the price of one."

"Huh?" Bryant's old doubts were reawakened. "Why should . . . ? Does that mean something can go wrong?"

Marzian laughed indulgently. "The Probability Redistributor *never* goes wrong, sir, but we provide the Triple Chance facility so that each client can select a reality which *exactly* matches his requirements. On the rare occasions when a problem arises, it is usually because the specification was incomplete or too vague."

"I see." Bryant tilted his head, frowning. "Or do I?"

Marzian spread his hands. "Well, suppose you were a poker fanatic and you asked to be relocated in a reality where everything – social status included – was dictated by skill in poker. When you got there you might find that the inhabitants of that universe played nothing but five-card draw, whereas your strong point was seven-card stud. That wouldn't be very satisfactory from your point of view, but all you would have to do would be to press the button on your handy pocket-sized Probability Normalizer, and it would instantly return you to this reality. Under the terms of our Triple Chance clause you would be entitled to a free transfer to a clearly specified universe where seven-card stud was the thing, and you would live happily ever after and Altereality Incorporated would have yet another satisfied client."

Bryant's brow cleared. "Nothing could be fairer than that! When can I go?"

"Almost immediately, sir. As soon as . . ." Marzian gave a polite but significant cough.

"There's no need to worry about the money side of it," Bryant said buoyantly. "I've got just over a hundred thou in my account. Mind you, I had to sell everything I owned to get it, but what the hell! The way I see it, if I'm not going to be back in this reality, I might as well . . ." He broke off as he noted the pained expression which had appeared on Marzian's face.

"If you would care to speak to Miss Cruft, she will deal with all the necessary formalities," Marzian said, sweeping one hand in the direction of the plump girl's desk. "In the meantime I will activate and calibrate the Probability Redistributor." He sat down at his own larger desk, which to Bryant's eyes now had something of the appearance of a console, and started clicking switches.

"Of course," Bryant said in an apologetic voice, sensing that the branch manager – as a professional rearranger of probabilities – was above concerning himself with the vulgar commercial details of the business. When he approached Miss Cruft her smile was sympathetic, and unexpectedly pleasant, but Bryant scarcely registered the fact. His thoughts were already turning to the lissome, long-thighed beauties who could be clamouring for his favours when he was the most perfectly developed man in the world. He established his identity and credit rating, made a computerised transfer of funds, and signed contractual papers in a haze of pleasurable anticipation.

"Here's your Probability Normalizer," Marzian said, handing him an object like a cigarette case with a press button in the centre of one side. "Now, if you would like to stand on the probability focus plate . . ."

Bryant obediently stepped on to the floor-mounted silver disk and watched Marzian rotate knobs and tap keys on panels that were let into his desk. At the conclusion of the ritual, Marzian reached for a red button which was larger than all the others. Bryant had time for one pang of wonderment and apprehension at the idea of being propelled into an alternative universe – then Marzian and Miss Cruft and all their familiar surroundings were gone.

He was standing in a vast, green-tiled plaza which was rimmed with egg-shaped buildings. Here and there were potted palms which swayed continuously despite the absence of any breeze, and the sun appeared to have spiral offshoots like a frozen Catherine wheel, but Bryant had no thought to spare for external marvels. First on the list of priorities was the checking out of his brand-new superbody; then would come a few weeks of silken dalliance; then perhaps he would get round to nature studies.

He looked down at himself – and emitted a bleat of anguish.

His physique had not changed in any way!

Whimpering with disappointment, he pulled off his jacket and shirt and confirmed the awful discovery that his body was the same substandard assemblage of frail bones and assorted scraps of fatty tissue he had always known. When he tried to flex his right bicep it, as always, continued to snuggle along his upper arm like two ounces of hog belly. Bryant was glowering at it, his disappointment turning to anger against T. D. Marzian and the criminal organisation for which he worked, when he heard a low whistle from somewhere close behind him.

"Take a gander at that physique," a man's voice said in tones of awe. "Say, I'll bet you that's Mister Galaxy."

"Nah," said another male voice. "Mister Galaxy can't match those deltoids – he must be Mister Cosmos."

Bryant whirled round, saw two oddly attired little men gaping at his torso and his rising fury spilled over into words. "Are you trying to be funny?" he demanded. "Because if you are . . ."

The little men cowered back with a convincing show of fear.

"Not us, sir," one of them babbled. "Forgive us for making comments, but we're both physical-culture freaks from way back, and we've never seen a human powerhouse like you before."

"That's right," his companion put in fervently. "I'd give a million zlinkots for a build like yours. *Two* million."

Bryant glared from one to the other, still convinced he was being hazed; then a curious fact was borne home to him. Malicious fate had saddled him with a body that was undersized and puny, but that was nothing to the trick it had played on these strangers. They barely came up to his shoulder, and their clinging garments revealed concave chests and legs which would have looked more appropriate on stick insects. Bryant looked beyond them and saw that all the other men strolling in the plaza were jerry-built on similar lines, and the first glimmers of understanding came to him.

If what he saw was a representative sample, if all the men on this world looked alike, then there was every likelihood that he *was* the most perfectly developed specimen of the lot.

Alterealities Incorporated had fulfilled its contract after all, but not in the way he had anticipated.

"I can't get over those pectorals," the first man commented, his gaze fixed admiringly on Bryant's chest.

"And how about those lats?" the second one added. "He must work out for *hours* every day."

"Oh, I like to keep in shape," Bryant said modestly, preening himself. Then a new thought came to him. "Do you think the girls would go for a body like mine?"

"Go for it!" The first man rolled his eyes. "You won't be able to fight them off."

As if to verify his words, there came a series of gasps, giggles and other sounds of feminine delight from somewhere off to Bryant's right. He turned and saw a group of six or seven young women approaching him at considerable speed. They were wide-eyed and pink-cheeked with what appeared to be unbridled desire. After a brief pause, during which they ogled his body from close up, they began to touch him with eager fingers. Others jostled for position, and in less than ten seconds Bryant was at the centre of a scrimmage. As he struggled to keep his feet in the confusion, hands clutched at various parts of his anatomy with disconcerting lack of finesse, bodies ground against him, lips were pressed urgently to his, and his ears were bombarded with proposals, the least bold of which required him to nominate his place or hers.

The situation might have been highly gratifying to one with Bryant's history of frustration, except for one unfortunate fact – the women of this world were, if anything, less well-endowed than their menfolk. Sharp elbows and knees beat painful tattoos all over his frame; bony fingers threated to remove pieces of his flesh. The overall effect was akin to being attacked by rapacious skeletons. Moaning in panic, Bryant lunged for freedom, groping in his jacket pocket for the flat shape of the Probability Normalizer.

He found it, pressed the button, and on the instant – his jacket and shirt still draped over his arm – he was standing on the silvery disk in Alterealities Incorporated's New York office. T. D. Marzian and Miss Cruft were gazing at him, the former with cool surprise, the latter with some degree of consternation.

"Were things not entirely to your satisfaction, sir?" Marzian asked blandly.

"Satisfaction?" Bryant quavered, heading unsteadily for the nearest chair. "My God, man, I nearly got torn to pieces!"

He began to relate what had happened, but had uttered only a few words when it came to him that he was partially nude in the presence of Miss Cruft. Embarrassed, he struggled into his clothing and finished his story.

"Most unfortunate," Marzian said in matter-of-fact tones. "But now you can appreciate the value of our Triple Chance facility – you still have two free transfers in hand."

"*Two*? You mean you're going to count that . . . shambles?" Bryant was shocked and indignant. "You sent me into a completely wrong sort of universe."

"It was the one you specified. We have your instructions here in your own writing."

"Yes, but when I said I wanted to be the most perfectly developed man in the world, I meant I wanted a new physique. One like Mister America's."

Marzian gave him a barely perceptible shake of the head. "The Probability Redistributor doesn't work that way. You are *you*, sir. You are one invariant point in an ocean of probabilities, and nothing can be done to alter that fact. The only realities in which you can exist are those in which you are short of stature and . . . um . . . somewhat underpowered."

Bryant, having invested practically every penny he owned, refused to be put off so easily. "Aren't there any realities in which all the men are scrawny midgets, like the two I told you about, and all the women are . . . well . . . normal?" Making sure Miss Cruft was not watching, Bryant made ballooning gestures in front of his chest so that there would be no doubt about what he meant by "normal".

"That's hardly logical, is it?" Marzian's voice now had an edge of impatience. "The males and females of any species have to be compatible, to share similar characteristics; otherwise that species couldn't exist."

Bryant's shoulders slumped. "Does that mean I've wasted all my money? All I wanted was to live in a reality where beautiful women would fall over themselves to get at me. Was that too much to ask?"

Marzian stroked his chin with the air of a man intrigued by a professional challenge. "There's no need to despair, Mr Bryant. Just take a look around you at our own reality. There are lots of extremely unprepossessing men who have more women than they know what to do with. The common factor is that these men can do something better than most others. Women go for success, you see. It doesn't have to be in anything marvellous – singing, dancing, hitting a ball, driving a car . . . Is there anything you are particularly good at?"

"I'm afraid not," Bryant said dolefully.

"Well, is there anything you are *fairly* good at?"

"Sorry." Bryant took his newly-signed contract from his pocket and began scanning the small print. "What's your policy about refunds?"

"How about acting? Or shooting pool?" Marzian was beginning to sound anxious. "Can't you even write stories?"

"No." Bryant shuffled the contract's pages, then paused with a sheepish expression on his face. "There was *one* thing I could do at school – better than anybody else – but it's too stupid for words."

"Try me," Marzian urged.

"Well . . ." Bryant gave him a tremulous smile. "I could blow bubbles off my tongue."

Marzian placed a hand on the nape of his neck and smoothed some hair down over his collar. "You could blow bubbles off your tongue."

"That's right," Bryant said with some signs of animation. "It's not as easy as you might think. You've got to work up the right sort of saliva – not too thick and not too thin – to form a durable bubble. Then you've got to direct your breath against it at exactly the right angle to separate it from the tip of your tongue –

not too high and not too low. And you have to curl your tongue into the right shape, as well. I was the only boy in my class who ever got four bubbles into the air at once."

"Really? Well, I suppose it's worth a try." Marzian tapped some keys on his desk, studied a visual display unit for a moment, then looked up at Bryant in round-eyed surprise. "This business never ceases to amaze me – there actually are other realities in which the principal glamour sport is skimming bubbles off the end of your tongue!"

"And the women are . . . normal?"

Marzian nodded. "We're talking about Sector One probabilities, which means that everything else is pretty much the same as it is here."

"Can you transfer me to one of them?" Bryant said, with an abrupt up-swing in his mood. "One where the all-time champ had never managed more than three bubbles in the air at once?"

"It's at the extreme range of the equipment, but I can do it." Marzian gestured in the direction of Miss Cruft. "You'll need to complete a new authorisation."

"Of course." When Bryant stooped over Miss Cruft's desk to fill in the necessary forms, he became aware that she used an extremely heady brand of perfume, but his mind was preoccupied with visions of the slim-waisted sirens who were to be in his ideal universe. He signed his name with a flourish and strode over to the probability focus plate.

"Good luck," Miss Cruft said.

Bryant scarcely heard her. He took up his position on the silver disk, folded his arms and watched Marzian's fingers flicker over the control panels as they tampered with the very structure of reality. Marzian concluded by hitting the red button and, as before, the transfer was instantaneous.

Bryant found himself standing in a busy street in what could have been Manhattan had the buildings been higher and the traffic a few decibels louder. The men and women who thronged the sidewalks appeared normal, and the styles of their clothing differed only slightly from those of the reality Bryant had left behind. He looked closely at passers-by and saw that many of them were attempting to blow bubbles off their tongues as they went about the day's business. Men and women alike were trying, and Bryant was gratified to see that not one of them had any vestige of style or technique. In his ten minutes of watching not one succeeded in launching a single bubble.

Feeling more than a little self-conscious, Bryant moved out of the doorway in which he had been sheltering and began flipping bubbles. His boyhood skills did not return immediately, but within a short time he had begun achieving good separations. Bubble after bubble was lobbed into quivering flight, and inevitably – in spite of the far from ideal conditions – there came a moment when he had two in the air at once. By then he was at the centre of a crowd of spectators, and the event was greeted with a rousing cheer. He nodded demurely, acknowledging the applause, and was heartened to see that quite a few of his audience were desirable women and that they were gazing at him with every sign of adoration.

This is more like it, he thought.

A gleaming chauffeur-driven limousine pulled up at the edge of the crowd. The fat man who got out of it was richly dressed and exuded an unmistakable aura of power. Bryant, aware of his scrutiny, speeded up his action and almost at once got three bubbles airborne. The crowd went wild. Car horns sounded as traffic began to jam the street.

"Say, are you a professional?" The fat man had somehow forced his way to Bryant's side. "What's your name?"

Bryant grinned up at him, intuitively sure of what was coming next. "Arthur Bryant, and I'm not a professional."

"You are now – I can get you a million shiller a contest." The fat man indicated his limousine. "Come on."

"With pleasure." Bryant struggled to the car in the wake of his benefactor, got in and found himself sharing the rear seat with two of the most stunning women he had ever seen.

"Girls, I'd like you to meet Arthur," the fat man said. "He's the next world champion bubbler, and I want you to be nice to him. *Real* nice. Got that?" The girls nodded in unison and turned to Bryant with slow-smouldering smiles which caused every nerve in his body to thrum like harp strings.

Bryant sat up in the huge circular bed, rearranged the black satin pillows to support his back, and stared moodily at the beautiful young woman who was lying beside him.

Three weeks had passed since he switched realities, and in that time he had become world champion in his chosen field, had made additional fortunes through endorsing a range of commercial products, had bought an island and a yacht, and had just signed up for his first three movies. He had also consorted with a succession of incredibly beautiful and passionate women, and many, many others were waiting in line just for the privilege of being seen with him.

By all his own estimates he should have been deliriously happy – but something had gone wrong with his dream world. Something he had not foreseen.

The young woman beside him opened her eyes, stirred languorously and said, "Do it again, Arthur."

Bryant shook his head. "I'm not in the mood."

"Go on, Arthur baby," she pleaded. "Just one more time."

He tightened his lips obstinately. The effort of flicking thousands of bubbles a day into the air had given him a painful blister where the underside of his tongue rubbed against his teeth. As a result he had had to modify his technique and flick much faster, and the associated hyperventilation gave him dizzy spells and nausea. Into the bargain, he was bored.

The girl purred sensuously and moved closer. "Just once more – just one little bubble."

Bryant put out his much-abused tongue and pointed at it angrily. "There's more to me than this thing, you know," he said with forgivable indistinctness. "I'm not just a tongue – I've got a *mind*. Doesn't it ever occur to anybody that I might want to discuss philosophy?"

The girl frowned. "Phil *who*?"

"That does it!" On impulse, Bryant snatched his Probability Normalizer from the bedside table and pressed the button. On

the instant, he was back in the Alterealities office, sprawling on
the floor under the startled gazes of T. D. Marzian and Miss
Cruft. The latter's face turned a becoming shade of pink.
Cursing himself for not having had the foresight to change out
of his silk *boudoir* suit, Bryant scrambled to his feet and took
shelter behind a chair while he adjusted what there was of his
clothing.

"It's been three weeks, Mr Bryant," Marzian said in neutral
tones, opening a closet door and taking out a dressing gown.
"Have we still got problems?"

"Problems!" Bryant accepted the gown and was slipping it on
when a new thought occurred to him. "You seem to have quite
a few of these things in there."

An indecipherable expression flitted across Marzian's face as
he removed the Probability Normalizer from Bryant's unresist-
ing fingers and dropped it into his own pocket. "Other clients
have returned on the spur of the moment. Were things getting
tiresome?"

"Tiresome isn't the word for it," Bryant said, grateful for an
understanding ear. "You have no idea what it's like to be
treated as an unfeeling object, to have people simply making
use of you night and day."

"That was the reality you specified."

"Yeah, but I didn't *understand*. What I really needed was a
universe where I would be appreciated for myself, for the real
me, as a thinking person."

"And are you?"

"Am I what?"

"A thinking person?"

Bryant scratched his head. "I think so. I mean I go around
thinking all the time, don't I?"

"You picked the wrong reality twice in a row."

"Ah, but that was because I didn't think." Bryant narrowed
his eyes, suspecting the other man was trying to make him look
stupid. "I've thought the whole thing over – and I want you to
transfer me to a reality in which I'll be regarded as the wisest
man in the world."

"I'm afraid the Probability Redistributor can't cope with that sort of request," Marzian said. "The target is too vague, you see. So many people have different ideas as to what constitutes wisdom. If we tried to effect a transfer under those terms, you'd be diffused into thousands of different realities. You'd become a kind of statistical gas, and you don't really want that to happen."

Bryant considered the prospect for a moment. "You're right – so what can we do?"

"The trick is to particularise," Marzian replied with weary expertise. "You think up something really deep, and I'll incorporate it into the specification and transfer you to a reality where it's regarded as the wisest thing ever said. Do you see what I mean?"

"Of course I see what you mean."

"Go ahead then."

"I'm *going* to – it's just that . . ." Bryant's voice tailed off uncertainly as he came face to face with the realisation that it was much easier to proclaim oneself a thinker than to measure up to the job. "Well, it's just that . . ."

"We close in ten minutes," Marzian said unhelpfully. "Can't you think of anything?"

"Don't rush me." Bryant placed a hand on his brow and tried to concentrate. "Let me see now . . . something's coming . . ."

"Let's have it – I've got a train to catch."

"Okay, here goes." Bryant closed his eyes and began to intone in a hollow voice. "There's no point in fishing for truth unless you are using the right bait."

Marzian gave an unexpected bark of laughter which almost drowned out a low gurgle from Miss Cruft.

"What's the matter?" Bryant said, unnerved and deeply offended. "You think that's funny?"

"No, no – it's very . . . profound." Marzian dabbed something from one of his eyes. "Forgive me – I've been under a strain lately, and my nerves aren't too . . ." He cleared his throat and turned to the control panels on his desk. "Please step on to the probability focus plate and we'll proceed."

Bryant hesitated. "Don't I have to sign new papers?"

"Not this time," Marzian said carelessly, beginning to tap at his keyboards. "We like to get everything down in black and white for each client's first two transfers, just in case there's any quibbling afterwards, but this is your third shot – and this time you won't be coming back. Whatever reality you fetch up in, you're there for keeps."

"I see." Bryant, now older and wiser with regard to all the hazards of reality-switching, felt a sudden timidity about what he was proposing to do. His first two excursions into alternative universes had been disastrous, and this time there would be no prearranged escape hatch. He hung back for a moment, teetering, then noticed that Miss Cruft was observing his reactions with broody interest. Squaring his shoulders, he stepped on to the silver disk and nodded for Marzian to go ahead.

"Here we go," Marzian said as he finished keying in the new specification. "Good-bye and good luck!"

With a showman's flourish he brought his hand over the red button and pressed down hard.

Nothing happened.

Bryant, who had been unconsciously cringing, straightened up and watched attentively as Marzian pressed the button again and again. The familiar surroundings of the office refused even to waver. They remained solid, immutable, *real*.

"I can hardly believe this," Marzian exclaimed, his jowls turning a lighter shade of grey. "It's the very first time the Probability Redistributor has ever failed to . . . unless . . . Wait a minute!" He depressed a few keys, examined dials and instruments, and sat back in his chair looking thunderstruck.

"Fuse gone?" Bryant ventured, wishing he had a technical background.

"The capacitors are fully discharged," Marzian said. "The machine did everything it was supposed to do!"

Bryant had another look around the office, searching for small signs of change. "Does that mean we're all in a different reality?"

Marzian shook his head impatiently. "That can't happen. What it means is that there is somebody in our reality who actually thinks that dumb remark of yours about fishing for truth is the wisest thing ever said."

"But that's impossible! I only made it up a minute ago, so nobody could have . . ." Bryant's voice faded under the impact of a startling new thought. He turned to face Miss Cruft.

She lowered her gaze and began to blush.

"What have you *done*?" Bryant demanded, advancing on her. "You've wasted my third shot! At least, I think you've wasted my . . ." His voice trailed away again as it came to him that although Miss Cruft was undeniably plump, some parts of her were plumper than others, and concerning those Nature had made a judicious selection. She also had a charming smile and wore sexy perfume, but the thing that attracted Bryant most of all was Miss Cruft's intellect – not many girls could appreciate genuine wisdom when they heard it. Looking down at her, he found himself falling deeply and irrevocably in love.

"I can't apologize enough," Marzian said, still scrutinising his control panels. "Under the circumstances, I guess you're entitled to a fourth transfer free of charge."

"Forget it." Bryant was so elated that he was unable to resist composing another aphorism. "Far-off pastures are green with fool's gold."

The saying, even to his own ears, seemed to have a flaw somewhere, but the gratified smile it drew from Miss Cruft was assurance that she knew exactly what he meant, and that they were going to share a wonderful future in the best of all possible universes.

STORMSEEKER

For several moonspins now – like a field lying fallow, like a steel blade shedding its fatigue – I have been waiting and resting. But lately a sense of imminence has grown and I have taken to night-riding in the silent sled, soaring over the city's trembling lights or drifting low in a Debussy prelude ambience of moonlight and towers, fulfilling childhood dreams of flight. At times I hover close to stolid old buildings, filling my eyes with the details of their crenels and corbels, but such things look strangely ir-relevant when viewed from close anchorage on a tide of dark winds. They produce a sense of unease and vertigo, of a dangerous ending to the volant dream, and I turn the sled away, wondering what the birds must think of us.

Selena has gone with me on several of these aerial excursions, on nights when neither of us could sleep, yet I know they make her unhappy. Percipient to a wonderful degree though she is, a streak of practicality in her nature forces her to question my "profession". We talk about having children – I have been assured I will breed neither mooncalves nor mutants – and while she nods in agreement her eyes grow smoky with doubt. Who could blame her? Only I can sense the ethereal migration of electrons and scry the shadows of lightning flashes yet unborn.

It is coming at last – the first storm of the season.

Archbold called me this morning but I had been aware for hours and said so. Even had the weather satellites not fallen dumb in their orbits I would have been the first to know, I told him haughtily. But his sole concern, of course, was that I could deliver.

As a true child of World War Three Point Three Repeating, I feel sorry for Archbold. He sits there in his underground rooms like a mole, his whereabouts marked by that single steel mast and the blankets of meshed cable whose oxidation has done odd things to the colours of the surrounding vegetation. The same political and nuclear forces that brought me into being have reduced his kind to their present lowly station. Scientists are generally unloved but GlobeGov is too wise and experienced to ban their activities. All that was necessary was to withdraw fiscal and fiduciary support. Now Archbold, the archetypal physicist, languishes underground, dreaming of the 300GeV accelerator that has lapsed into decay at Berne and relying on biological sports like me.

If the truth were told, some of his colleagues would like to get me under the knife and probe for extra organs or neural abnormalities which might explain my existence. But even Archbold would never countenance dissection of a goose that lays a billion golden eggs in every clutch.

It is almost here, this first storm of the season, and I can sense its strength. All day warmly humid air has been streaming upward over the streets and quiet terraces of Brandywell Hill. Water from the sea, the river, the pale rectangular emeralds of the private pools has been swirling aloft into a white anvil of cloud ten miles high. Scrying into the misty universe of cumulo-nimbus I was able to "see" the moisture of its central up-seeking column condense and freeze into hailstones which, having strayed from the geometries of the normal world, were unable to fall. Dancing on the awesome chimney current, they rose higher and higher until the force of the current was exhausted, then spewed out in all directions, carrying cold air down with them. And as the vast process continued my excitement grew, for the electrons within that cloud had begun their inexplicable migration to its base. Up there, not far above the coping stones of the city's towers, they gather like spermatozoa – and their combined pressure grows as irresistible as the force of life itself.

Selena sees nothing of this – but I am delirious with pleasure over the fact that, for the first time, she is accompanying me to meet a storm. Tonight I will be able to make her feel with my senses, let her know what it is like to ride herd on a billion times a billion elementary particles. Tonight I will drink fulfilment from her eyes. Our sled soars high in the fretful air. Selena lies, pale and nostalgic, in the cup beside me as the shivering craft describes slow circles in the darkening sky. But for once my eyes are elsewhere.

"Look, my darling." I point down to the patient, shimmering lights of an isolated suburb glowing broochlike in the shape of an anchor.

She looks over the edge and her face is expressionless. "I see nothing."

"There's nothing for your eyes to see – yet – but a ghost is slipping through those houses." I pick up the sled's microphone. "Are you ready, Archbold?"

"We're ready," his voice crackles from the darkness trapped in the hollow of my hand.

"In less than a minute," I say, setting the microphone down. This is where my work begins. I try to explain it to Selena. Above us the cloud is tumescent with electrons as its incredible negative charge increases, and on the ground beneath it an equally great positive charge is formed like an image in a mirror. As the cloud drifts, the earth's positive charge – a shadow only I can "see" – follows it, hopefully seeking its own fulfilment.

The image glides silently and eagerly across the ground, climbing trees, scaling the mossy steeples and towers. It races into houses and ascends water pipes, television antennae, lightning conductors, anything that can bring it closer to its elusive cloud-borne partner. And none of the people and dreaming children and watchful animals can even feel its transient, engulfing presence.

Suddenly Selena is sitting upright – the electrical potential has come so close to orgasm-point that it manifests itself to normal senses. A thin white arm reaches down from the base of the cloud.

"Archbold calls that a leader," I say through dry lips. "A gaseous arc path, reacting to electricity like the gas in a neon tube."

"It seems to be searching for something." Her voice is small and sad.

I nod abstractedly, spreading the net of my mind, once again awed at my power to control – even briefly – the unthinkable forces gathering around us. To our right the leader hangs, hesitating a moment, thickening and brightening as the electrons in the cloud swarm into it. Then it reaches down again, extending to several times its former length, I glance toward the ground and realise it is time for me to act. The activity of the positive particles on earth has increased to the point where streamers of St. Elmo's fire are snaking upward from the highest points. Yearning arms stretch from the tops of steeples. At any second one of them will contact the down-seeking leader – and when that happens lightning will stalk the brief pathway between earth and sky.

"I see it," Selena breathes. "I live."

At that moment I strike with my brain, exerting that miraculous power, that leverage which can be obtained only when one's neural system branches into crevices in another continuum. The leader, flame-bright now, changes direction and moves southward to where Archbold is waiting in his underground rooms. On the ground beneath it the positive image also changes course, its white streamers reaching higher, in supplication, in – love.

"Now, Archbold," I whisper into the microphone. "Now!"

His telescopic steel mast, driven by explosives, spears up into the sky and penetrates the leader, absorbing its charge. The ground image leaps forward eagerly but its streamers are sucked down as it encounters Archbold's carefully spread blankets of steel mesh. Both charges – cloud-borne negative and earth-bound positive – flow down massive cables. In an instant their energy is expended, far below ground, in one of the experiments with which Archbold hopes to achieve a true understanding of the nature of matter by accelerating particles to speeds far greater than they ever achieve in nature. At this moment, however, I am not concerned with the physicist's philosophical absurdities and arcana.

"They've gone," Selena says. "What happened?"

I hold the sled on its course with unsteady hands. "I delivered the power of a lightning strike to Archbold, as I promised."

She examines me with dismayed eyes, her face a calm goddess-mask in the instrument lights.

"You enjoyed it."

"Of course."

"You enjoyed it too much."

"I – I don't understand." As always, a strange sad weakness is spreading through my limbs.

"I won't give you children," she says, with the peacefulness of utter conviction. "You have no instinct for life."

The storm season is almost over now. I have not seen Selena since that night and I often muse about why she left me. She was right about the nature of my work, of course. There would be no vegetation or animals or human beings on Earth were lightning not there to transform atmospheric nitrogen into soil-nourishing nitric acids. And so by diverting the great discharges into Archbold's lair I am, in a very small way, opposing my mind and strength to the global tides of life itself. But I suspect that my infinitesimal effect on the biosphere is of no concern to Selena. I suspect she has a more immediate, more personal reason for rejecting me.

There is no time to think about such things now, though. Another storm is coming, perhaps the last of the season – and I must fly to meet it.

ALIENS AREN'T HUMAN

"What a beautiful day!" Kston said in his thin, lisping voice. "How pleasant to be at peace with the cosmos, and to enjoy the companionship of good friends! How wonderful it is to be alive on such a day!"

That was five seconds before the car hit him.

President Johnny Ciano, who was walking across the plaza with the little Dorrinian diplomat, saw the speeding vehicle first. It registered at the edge of his vision as a silver-blue shape which was changing its position with unusual rapidity, and the instinct for self-preservation – ever strong in his family – prompted him to check his stride. The car had swung off the street which formed the plaza's southern boundary and was hurtling between an ornamental fountain and a soft drinks stand at over a hundred, its magnetic engine emitting an angry whine.

Ciano's immediate thought was that the vehicle had gone out of control, then he made out the figure of his own cousin – Frankie Ritzo – crouched over the steering wheel, his eyes gleaming like miniature versions of the car's headlights.

The fool! Ciano thought, turning to warn Kston. The grey-skinned alien had moved ahead of him, oblivious to all danger, and was still prattling happily about the joys of existence when the car swatted him skywards in a parabola which would have cleared a large house. At the top of its trajectory his body struck the outflung arm of a bronze statue, one of a symbolic group, bending it to an unfortunate position in which its owner appeared to be fondling the left breast of the Mother of Creation. Still spinning, the alien's compact form came down on a marble bench – converting it to a heap of expensive rubble – bounced twice and rolled to a halt amid a knot of elderly female shoppers, several of whom began screaming. The car which had initiated the grotesque sequence slewed its way across the plaza and disappeared into a narrow street on the west side.

"Holy Mary," Ciano sobbed, running towards the fallen body. "This is terrible! Send for a priest, somebody."

"A priest will be no use for this job," Kston said, springing to his feet and picking up a piece of the shattered bench. "Unless, of course, your clergy also serve as stone-masons. Forgive this humble being for not being familiar with human . . ."

"I'm not talking about the bench." Ciano gaped at the diplomat's grey hide which was unmarked and miraculously intact.

"The statue, then." Kston looked up at the metal sculptures. "This humble being considers that the arrangement has been improved. It's more symbolic than ever, if you know what this humble being means."

"I'm talking about *you*, Kston – I thought you were dead."

"Dead?" Kston closed one eye, which was his way of showing puzzlement. "How could this humble being die while he is still young?"

"That car was doing at least a hundred when it hit you. I don't know what you must think of us, Kston, but you can rest assured that no effort will be spared in the search for the driver. We'll find him no matter how long it takes, and when we do . . ."

"But this humble being thought your cousin was joining us for lunch?" Kston said mildly.

"My cousin?" Ciano felt both his knees partake of a loose circular motion. "You saw the driver?"

"Yes. It was your cousin Frankie, the Secretary for External Affairs."

Ciano stared numbly at Kston, and then at the shoppers who had sorted themselves out and were beginning to take an interest in the conversation. "Let's move on," he said hastily, his brain racing as he tried to think of a way out of the situation in which his cousin's assassination attempt had placed him. Ritzo's lack of finesse had always made him something of an embarrassment to the government of New Sicily, but with this latest piece of crassness he had become a downright liability. Ciano made up his mind that Ritzo would have to be sacrificed, that he was prepared to go as far as a public execution if it would save the top-level talks.

"Are you positive it was Secretary Ritzo?" He made a last effort to save his cousin's life. "I mean, there are lots of cars just like that one."

"It was Frankie, all right." Kston showed his slate-like teeth. "This humble being can see why you put him in charge of External Affairs. It is rare for anybody to show such considera- tion for a visitor. His car obviously was not designed for playing boost-a-body, and yet he went right ahead and boosted this humble being. He just didn't care how much damage would be done to his vehicle . . . and this humble being finds that really heart-warming. Don't you?"

"Aw . . . ah," Ciano said. Even to his own ears the comment seemed to lack incisiveness, but for the moment he was unable to improve on it.

"It's obvious that Frankie has studied Dorrinian customs and has learned that boost-a-body is one of our favourite games. It was a nice diplomatic gesture, but . . ." Kston smiled his dark smile again. "This humble being is afraid it doesn't change his mind about our heavy mineral deposits."

"I need a drink," Ciano mumbled. He escorted Kston across the street and into the hotel, owned by his uncle, which had the catering contracts for the Department of Trade. They went straight into the VIP bar, a large room decorated in Earth-style traditional, complete with a high-mounted television set showing sports programmes. Ciano ordered two triple whiskies. While the drinks were being served he covertly examined the Dorrin- ian, whose physique could best be described as pyramidic humanoid. The grey-skinned body grew steadily wider and thicker from the top of a bald, pointed head to the short, immensely powerful legs which ended in slab-like feet. Kston was nude, but this condition was acceptable to human eyes, partly because his genitals were internal, partly because his smooth hide created the impression he was dressed in a one- piece garment of supertuff.

Ciano examined that hide carefully while sipping his drink and was unable to detect the slightest sign of lacerations or bruises resulting from impacts which would have burst a human body like a ripe tumshi fruit. He guessed that the high gravity on Kston's home world had led to the evolution of incredibly robust inhabitants; and from there his thoughts went on to the fact that Dorrin was also the only planet in the local system with an adequate supply of elements heavier than iron. Proper development of New Sicily was impossible without access to those elements, but the Dorrinians were adamant about refusing mining rights.

"Listen, Kston," he said, adding generous quantities of warmth and sincerity to his voice, "there must be *something* here on New Sicily that your people would like to have."

Kston blinked to signify agreement. "Indeed yes. Sulphur in particular is prized by our chefs as a condiment, but our supplies are almost exhausted."

"Then we should be able to work out an exchange deal."

"This humble being fears not. The word 'exchange' implies the existence of two parties, each of which is the sole owner of a commodity."

Ciano weighed up the comment and failed to see its point. "Well?"

"Well, the Dorrinian viewpoint is that, as this planetary system was our home for millions of years before the first ships arrived from Earth, every resource of every planet in it automatically belongs to us." The alien diplomat experimentally squeezed the chromed steel rail on the edge of the bar between finger and thumb, producing noticeable dents in it. "We don't feel disposed towards trading our own property in exchange for our own property."

"But you didn't have the necessary space technology until we gave it to you."

"It would have been developed," Kston said matter-of-factly. "In any case, this planet is more than adequate recompense for a little technical know-how."

Ciano smiled to conceal a pang of irritation and anger. The

Dorrinian made a great show of being humble and sweetly reasonable, but underneath he was a stubborn and bloody-minded monstrosity who deserved to be fitted with concrete boots and sent for a walk on a riverbed. The trouble was, Ciano was beginning to suspect, that were he to arrange such an excursion the alien actually would go for a submarine stroll and then come up smiling.

Taking a hefty swig of his drink, Ciano saw that Kston's attention had been drawn by a burst of cheering from the television set behind the bar. A heavyweight boxing match was in progress on the screen and the ringside crowd was erupting with excitement as one of the fighters, a giant in blue shorts, moved in for a devastating finish. He drove his opponent on to the ropes with a flurry of body blows, stepped back and caught him on the rebound with a right cross to the chin which landed with such leathery finality that, in spite of his preoccupations, Ciano winced in sympathy. The recipient went down on the instant, obviously unconscious before he hit the canvas, and lay like a side of bacon while the victor danced around him.

"This humble being fails to understand," Kston said. "What is happening?"

Ciano put down his empty glass. "It's a sport we humans call boxing. The idea is to . . ."

"The general idea is clear – we have a similar sport called dent-a-body – but why is that man pretending to sleep?"

"You mean you don't . . . ?" Ciano was wondering how he could explain the effects of a knock-out blow to the likes of Kston when his thoughts were diverted to a more serious problem – namely that of staying alive. A door at the rear of the large room crashed open, there were shouts and screams of panic, and in a mirror Ciano glimpsed his cousin Frankie – the Secretary for External Affairs – brandishing a demolisher. Ciano dropped to the floor with reflexive speed and crouched there, praying and swearing with equal fervour, while the weapon created its own version of hell. Blinding laser bursts seared the air and from the gun's multiple barrels, firing at the rate of a hundred rounds a second, came sprays of high-velocity bullets – some of them explosive, some armour-piercing – converging on the sites of the laser strikes. For a brief moment Ciano saw the stubby outline of the Dorrinian at the terrible focus of the destruction – limned in radiant blue fire – then there was comparative silence, the only sounds being those of tinkling glass and fleeing footsteps.

Trying to control the trembling of his limbs, Ciano struggled to stand up, already rehearsing the disclaimer he would have to issue to the news media. *I know the preliminary trade negotiations with the Dorrinian envoy were going badly, but that doesn't mean my family was involved with his assassination. We are men of honour, not . . . not . . .*

His thoughts dissolved into a confused blur as he saw that Kston was not only still on his feet, but apparently totally unharmed. The alien's grey hide was, if anything, smoother than before, and the hand with which he helped Ciano to his feet was steady. Ciano began to feel ill.

"This humble being fears that your cousin has gone too far this time," Kston said.

"You're so right," Ciano gritted. "I promise you he'll pay for this."

"The expense will be considerable." Kston surveyed the shattered and smoking ruins of the bar counter. "Obviously Frankie learned about the Dorrinian custom of ablate-a-body – in which a thoughtful host refreshes a guest by scouring off the outer layer of dead skin cells – but it is usually done in special cubicles where there can be no damage to the surroundings. Perhaps your cousin got carried away in his eagerness to be hospitable."

Ciano nodded, forcing his brain into action. "Frankie always was the cordial type. Look, Kston, can we go back to my office where it's quiet and get on with the talks?"

"Of course!" Kston showed his dark teeth. "This humble being can't imagine how you intend to negotiate from a position of such weakness, but he will be privileged to watch you try. Perhaps he will learn something."

"Hope so." Ciano spent a minute with the hotel manager, pacifying him by undertaking to foot all repair bills, then returned to his alien companion. "Let's go – this place looks like there's been a war."

"War? Is that your word for ablate-a-body?"

"I suppose you could say that," Ciano replied absently, his mind filled with the need to get hold of his wayward cousin and talk to him about his activities before something went seriously wrong. Ciano had no moral objections to murdering Kston – in fact, the more time he spent with the obsequious little alien the more attractive the idea seemed – but New Sicily was a recently formed colony, with severely limited military resources, and dared not antagonise the heavily populated neighbouring world of Dorrin. Secretary Ritzo was fully aware of the situation, which made his failed assassinations puzzling as well as embarrassing.

As soon as they were back in the Department of Trade building Ciano handed his guest over to the care of an assistant and went looking for Ritzo. He found him slumped over the bar in his private suite, drinking imported grappa straight from the bottle, his face several shades paler than usual.

"I got the shock of my life when I saw you coming back across the square with that . . . with that . . ." Unable to find a suitable epithet, Ritzo again raised the bottle with a trembling hand. "Didn't I even scratch him?"

"Just about," Ciano said. "Luckily for you, he enjoys being scratched."

"I tell you, Johnny, that guy ain't human."

"Of course he isn't human – that's what being an alien *means*!" Ciano snatched the bottle from his cousin's grasp and dropped it into a waste bin. "And there's a couple of billion more where he comes from. Have you any idea what the Dorrinians would have done to us if by some chance you had managed to rub out their representative?"

"Nothing."

"Precisely! And that's why you've got to . . . What do you mean nothing?"

A look of furtive triumph appeared on Ritzo's narrow face. "Some egghead in my department finally managed to translate those old Dorrinian books – you know the stuff that's been gathering dust since the cultural exchange way back in '22. One of them is a history book, Johnny, and d'you know what?"

"What?"

"The Dorrinians are total pacifists. Their written history goes back about twenty thousand years and they ain't never had a war in all that time! These guys are so pacifist that they don't have no armies or navies. They don't have no weapons of any kind."

"Maybe they don't need them."

"That's not it, Johnny. They believe that *everything* can be settled by talking if they stick at it long enough. One of their conferences went on for over a hundred years – and that was just to decide on the height of streetlamps! We don't have that sort of time."

Ciano nodded. "So what do you propose?"

"A bit of old-style persuasion, is all. We send the little creep back where he came from in a wooden box and tell the Dorrinians they're all gonna get the same treatment if they tries to interfere with our mining crews."

"Mmmm." Ciano stroked his jaw thoughtfully. "Not much finesse."

"Johnny, this is not time to go soft."

"Softness doesn't come into it. It's just that we have Kston here and we can talk to him. I think it would be better to make our intentions clear, then send him back to spread the word."

"I guess you're right." Ritzo's reluctant expression gave way to one of relief. "I was gonna try him with a bomb next, but it might have taken a tactical nuke."

As the sole representative of his planet, Kston had one side of the long conference table to himself. Opposite him were Ciano and Ritzo, accompanied by six other members of New Sicily's ruling family, including the hulking form of Mario Vicenzi, Secretary for War. The broad smile with which he faced the group indicated that, far from feeling overwhelmed, Kston was enjoying the prospect of a tough negotiating session.

"This humble being is flattered by the presence of so many illustrious humans, and he will do his utmost to justify the honour," he said. "Now that formal talks are about to begin, I propose that New Sicily should make a detailed presentation of its proposals. Twenty days should be sufficient for that phase of the talks, but I will not object to your taking longer as long as I am permitted equal time for my preliminary rejection of all your suggestions. As soon as each side has stated its position we can allocate, say, twenty days for debate on each point that we . . ."

"Pardon me for interrupting," Ciano said firmly, "but we're not going to bother with all that time-wasting crap."

Kston's smile faded. "Crap? This humble being doesn't understand."

"I'll explain. Starting tomorrow, we are going to send mining equipment and crews to your planet and we're going to take all the minerals we need. And if anybody tries to stop us we will drop thermonuclear bombs on your cities and large numbers of your people will be vaporised."

"Vaporised?" Kston gazed solemnly into Ciano's eyes. "You mean they would be . . . dead?"

"Very." Ciano felt an uncharacteristic twinge of pity as he noted the stunned expression on Kston's face. "You can't *get* any more dead than they would be." To his left the Secretary for War made an involuntary growling sound.

"But this is unfair! Unethical! If you are really prepared to do such a thing there is no point at all in discussing, debating, conferring, negotiating . . ."

"That's what we like about our system," Ciano put in. "Now, do you agree to give us unlimited mining rights?"

"This humble being has no other option," Kston said faintly, rising to his feet. "This has been a great shock – twenty thousand years of tradition swept away in a few seconds – but this humble being will return to his people immediately and explain the new situation."

"There's no need to go this very minute." Ciano stood up too, wishing the little alien had turned nasty instead of accepting the ultimatum so meekly. "After all, now that we understand each other there's no reason why we can't go on being good friends. Stay and share a bottle of wine with us while your ship is being readied."

"Perhaps that is a good idea." Kston summoned up a tremulous smile. "This humble being should try to get *something* out of the agreement."

Ciano and Ritzo led the laughter which greeted the alien's remark. Amid a sudden hubbub of good cheer the group, some of whom were slapping Kston's back, moved to the refreshments table at the end of the conference room. Red wine was decanted in generous quantities and somebody conjured up appropriately festive music.

"That went off easier than I expected," Ciano whispered to Ritzo. "I've never seen anybody cave in so fast."

"That's the way them Dorrinians is made," Ritzo said contemptuously. "I told you, fighting is unknown to them. They ain't got the spunk for it. No manliness. No pride. Watch this."

"Maybe you should leave well enough alone." Ciano tried to restrain his cousin, but was too late to prevent him sauntering over to Kston with a condescending grin.

"Drink a toast to eternal friendship," Ritzo said with an insulting lack of sincerity, raising his glass.

"To eternal friendship," Kston replied submissively, raising his glass.

"My little grey *amico*!" Ritzo bellowed, wine glistening on his chin as he gave Kston a resounding slap on the back.

"My large pink *amico*!" Kston lifted his free hand and, before Ciano could react to the sudden clamour of alarms in his head, used it to slap Ritzo's back. The effect was instantaneous and dramatic. The force of the blow, in addition to snapping Ritzo's spine, propelled him across the room and into a sickening impact with a marble column which became liberally smeared with blood as he slid down it. To all but one of the assembly it was obvious that Ritzo was dead.

"Why is my friend Frankie lying on the floor?" Kston piped, breaking the abrupt silence which had descended.

Secretary Vicenzi knelt beside the body and prodded it

tentatively, then looked up at Kston with an ominous coldness in his yellowish eyes. "Because you killed him."

"*Killed* him! But that is impossible. All this humble being did was . . ." Kston stared at his hand in perplexity for a moment, then raised his gaze to take in the intent group of humans. There was a look of dawning wonderment in his pebble-like eyes, a look which produced an icy sensation of dread in Ciano's gut.

"We take you to our bosoms as a trusted friend," Vicenzi rumbled, rising to his feet as he slid his hand into the inside pocket of his jacket. "And this is how you repay us!"

"But this humble being can't believe that humans can be so frail," Kston said, almost to himself. "You are so big, so aggressive that one naturally assumes . . ."

"I'll show you aggressive," Vicenzi interrupted as he produced an antique bone-handled cut-throat razor, a favourite weapon from his early days, and advanced on Kston. "I will also show you the colour of your own liver."

"That would be most interesting," Kston said politely, "but first this humble being must conduct a small experiment." Moving with frightening speed, he grasped Vicenzi's lapels in his left hand, pulling the big man down to his level, and slapped sideways with his right. There was an immediate fountaining of blood and something heavy struck the wall, bounced off and rolled underneath the conference table. Ciano, who had closed his eyes, knew without being told that it was Vicenzi's head, a conclusion which was verified by the hoarse cries of dismay from the remaining onlookers.

He also understood, belatedly and with a terrible clarity, that he and Ritzo and the others had made a lethal error of judgement concerning the Dorrinians. Men had been partial to the use of violence ever since the first distant ancestor had used a club to settle a dispute, but there had been one necessary underlying condition – among mankind violence *worked*. There were, thanks to design deficiencies in the human physique, dozens of quick and comparatively simple ways in which a critic or an opponent could be rendered silent and ineffective, either temporarily or permanently. It was natural therefore that the more pragmatic of the species should exploit the situation, but the Dorrinians – as Ciano had observed – were virtually indestructible. Far back in their history individuals had probably experimented with clubs, knives and bullets, found them totally ineffective, and in consequence had been forced to accept that the only way to resolve differences was by means of discussion.

From Ciano's point of view the sudden insight was cause for deep anxiety, but there was an even more disturbing factor to consider. Over the millennia man had developed a thing called a conscience, that inner voice which tempered his urge to kill off all who displeased him, thus making it possible for even the most violent to live in association with their fellows. Kston, however, was like a child who was enraptured with a brand-new plaything . . .

"I've been thinking things over, Kston," Ciano announced, trying to keep his voice steady. "It occurs to me that we have been unreasonable in our demands – I think it only fair that we should have further talks."

"This humble being has also been thinking things over, and he has an even better idea," Kston said, tossing Vicenzi's body into a far corner of the room. "My people can have as much sulphur as they want from this world – all this humble being has to do is kill the humans who would try to object. It's so *simple*."

"You can't do that," Ciano said, his mouth going dry.

"No? Watch this." In a single blurring movement Kston sprang at the two men nearest him, leaping high to bring him above their shoulders and striking down on their heads with both fists. They dropped to the floor with concave skulls impacted into their collar bones.

"What I mean," Ciano mumbled, cowering back, "Is that even if you killed everybody in this room you wouldn't have gained anything. There will always be others to take our places. I mean, there's a whole city out there . . . with thousands and thousands of human settlers in it . . . and you would have to kill every one of them."

"But, Johnny! That's exactly what this humble being intends to do!" Smiling his dark grey smile, the black cabochons of his eyes gleaming with ingenuous pleasure, the Dorrinian envoy went to work.

LOVE ME TENDER

It's a funny thing – I can think all right, but I can't think about the future. Tomorrow doesn't seem to exist for me any more. There's only today, and this drowsy, dreamy acceptance.

Most of the time it's cool here in the shack, the mosquito screens are holding together fairly well, and the bed is a whole lot better than some of the flea pits I've been in lately.

And she waits on me hand and foot. Couldn't be more attentive. Brings me food and drink – all I can stomach – and cleans me up afterwards. Even when I wake up during the night I can see her standing at the door of the room, always watching, always waiting.

But what's she waiting for? That's what I ask myself every so often, and when I do . . .

The swamp buggy had started off life as an ordinary Volkswagen, a beetle convertible, but somebody had extended the axles and fitted pudgy aircraft tyres which spread the vehicle's weight sufficiently to keep it from sinking in mud. Snow chains had been wrapped around the tyres to provide traction. The buggy was noisy, ungainly and uncomfortable, but it was able to negotiate the narrow tracks that ran through the Everglades, and Joe Massick felt it had been well worth the trouble he had taken to steal it.

He sat upright at the wheel, glancing over his shoulder every now and again as though expecting to see a police helicopter swooping down in pursuit, but the sky remained a featureless grey void. The air was hot and so saturated with water that it reminded him of the atmosphere inside the old-fashioned steam laundry where he had once worked as a boy. He did his best to ignore the sweat which rolled down his slab-like body, concentrating his attention on maintaining a north-westerly course in the general direction of Fort Myers.

His best chance of avoiding capture lay in making a quick crossing of the Florida peninsula without being seen, but it was beginning to dawn on him that the journey was not one to be undertaken lightly. The sloughs and swamps of the northern Everglades made up one of the last truly wild regions of the country, and as a confirmed town-dweller he felt threatened by every aspect of the flat and prehistoric landscape through which he was travelling. For the past thirty minutes he had been encountering stands of lifeless trees draped with Spanish moss, and now the intervals between the trees were growing so brief that he appeared to be entering a dead forest which provided a habitat for countless varieties of birds, insects and reptiles. The sound of the buggy's engine was almost drowned by the protests of the colonies of birds it disturbed, and on all sides there was a furtive agitation of other life forms, a sense of resentment, of being scrutinised and assessed by primeval eyes.

It was a feeling which Massick disliked intensely, prompting him to seek reassurance from the buggy's fuel gauge. The position of the needle showed that he still had three-quarters of a tank – more than enough, even allowing for forced detours, to take him to the far side of Big Cypress. He nodded, relaxing slightly into the burlap-covered seat, and had driven for perhaps another minute when a disturbing thought lodged itself like a pebble in the forefront of his mind.

According to the fuel gauge the tank had been three-quarters full when he first set out in the buggy almost an hour earlier. An optimist might have concluded that the vehicle's modest engine was using practically no gasoline, but Massick was beyond such naïvety. He tapped the gauge with his knuckles and saw that the needle was immovable, locked in place.

Doesn't prove a thing, he thought, vainly trying to sell himself the idea. *For all I know, the tank was filled right up*.

A mile further along the track, as he had known in his heart it was bound to do, the engine cut without even a preliminary cough. Massick turned the steering wheel and brought the buggy to rest in a thicket of saw grass and huge ferns. He sat for a moment with his head bowed, whispering the same swear word over and over again until it came to him that he was wasting precious time. The girl back in West Palm Beach might have died – he had been forced to hit her pretty hard to keep her quiet – but if she was still alive she would have given his description to the police and they would have connected him with the one in Orlando and the other one up in Fernandino. In any case, there was no time for sitting around feeling sorry for himself.

Massick picked up the plastic shopping bag which contained all his belongings, stepped down from the buggy, squelched his way back on to the trail and began walking. The surface was better for walking on than he had expected – probably owing its existence to the oil prospecting that had been carried out in the area some years earlier – but it soon became apparent that he was not cut out for trekking across swamps. He had been desperately tired to start off with, and before he had taken a dozen paces his clothes were sopping with perspiration, binding themselves to his well-larded body, maliciously hampering every movement. The air was so humid that he felt himself to be drinking with his lungs.

Now that he was proceeding without the roar of an engine and the clatter of chains, the swamp seemed ominously quiet and again he had the impression of being watched. The profusion of tree trunks and the curtains of hanging moss made it difficult to see far in any direction, and for all he knew he could have been accompanied by a stealthy army whose members were waiting until he collapsed with exhaustion before closing in. Childish though the fantasy was, he was unable to dismiss it completely from his mind and occasionally as he walked he fingered the massy solidity of the .38 pistol in his bag. The sky sagged close overhead, heavy with rain.

Two hours later he crossed one of the innumerable small concrete bridges which carried the track over dark streams and found that it forked in two directions, both of them uninviting to an equal degree. The sun had been invisible all along, and now that dusk was falling Massick's rudimentary trail sense was totally unable to cope with the task of identifying the branch which lay closest to the north-westerly course he wanted. He paused, breathing heavily, and looked around him in the tree-pillared gloom, suddenly understanding why in local Indian legend the big swamp was regarded as the home of ancestral spirits. It was easy to see the ghosts of dead men standing in slim canoes, drifting in silence through the endless colonnades and caverns.

The realisation that he was going to have to spend the night in such surroundings jerked Massick out of his indecision. He chose the right-hand path and moved along it at an increased pace, looking out for a hillock of any description upon which he would have a reasonable chance of remaining dry while he slept. It was only when he recalled that snakes also had a preference for high ground, especially in the wet season, that he admitted to himself the seriousness of his situation. He had no real idea how far he was from the townships of the west coast, and even if he did succeed in making his way through Big Cypress on foot he was going to emerge looking conspicuously bearded and filthy – the sort of figure that any cop would want to interrogate on sight.

The thought of being caught and put back in prison after less than a month of freedom caused Massick to give an involuntary moan. He reached into the plastic bag, took out the bottle of rum he had acquired at the same time as the swamp buggy and drank the few ounces of neat liquor it contained. The rum was warm and had an aftertaste of burnt brown sugar which made him wish he had a full fifth for solace during the approaching night. He hurled the bottle away, heard it come down with a splash and on the instant a cicada began to chirp nearby as though he had startled it into life. Within seconds a hundred others had taken up the chorus, walling him in with sound, advertising his presence for the benefit of any creature – human or inhuman – which might be lurking in the encompassing darkness. Startled, prey to fears he was unable to acknowledge, he quickened his pace even though each passing minute made the track more difficult to see. He was beginning to contemplate retracing his steps to the last concrete bridge when a yellow glow sprang into existence some distance ahead and slightly to his left.

Convinced for the moment that he had seen the headlights of an approaching vehicle, Massick snatched his pistol out of the bag, then realised there were no mechanical sounds such as another swamp buggy would have made. Keeping the gun at the ready, he went forward until he reached a barely discernible side track which branched off to the left and seemed to lead straight towards the glimmer of light. All the indications were that, against the odds, he had found some kind of habitation in the heart of the swamp.

The pang of pleasure and relief Massick experienced was not quite enough to obliterate his natural wariness. The only reason he could envisage for people living in the waterlogged wilderness was that they were wardens for one of the area's wildlife sanctuaries – and, for him, walking into an official establishment which had radio equipment could be as disastrous as calling in at the police station. He threaded his way along the path, trying not to make any sound as he negotiated successive barriers of dark vegetation, and after several minutes reached a hummock upon which was perched a wooden shanty. The wan radiance which seeped from the windows and the screen door was swallowed up by the surrounding blackness, but there was enough refraction to show that the building had been constructed from second-hand timbers – which pretty well ruled out the possibility of it being an outpost of authority. Emboldened by what he had found thus far, Massick crossed a cleared area to the nearest window and cautiously looked through it.

The room beyond the smeared glass was lit by oil lanterns hanging from hooks in the ceiling. Much of the floor space was taken up with stacks of cardboard boxes, and in the centre of the room was a rough wooden table at which sat a small stoop-shouldered man of about sixty. He had cropped grey hair, a sprinkling of silver stubble around his chin, and tiny crumpled ears which gave the impression of being clenched like fists. He was dressed in well-worn slacks and a faded green beach shirt. On the table before him was a bottle of whisky and several glass jars containing what looked like small twists of coloured paper. He was preoccupied with removing the coloured objects from the jars and carefully placing them in individual plastic boxes, pausing now and then to swig whisky straight from the bottle.

The room had two interior doors, one of them leading into a primitive kitchen. The other door was closed, but Massick guessed it led into the bedroom. He remained at the window long enough to assure himself that the occupant of the shanty was alone, then slipped the pistol into his side pocket, walked quietly to the screen door and tapped on it. The mosquito mesh made a noise like distant thunder. A few seconds later the small man appeared with a flashlight which he shone on Massick's face.

"Who's out there?" he growled. "Whaddaya want?"

"I got stranded," Massick explained, enduring the searching brilliance. "I need shelter for the night."

The man shook his head. "I got no spare room. Go away."

Massick opened the door and went inside, crowding the other man back. "I don't need much room, and I'll pay you twenty dollars for the night."

"What's the idea? What makes you think you can just walk in here?"

For a reply Massick used a trick he had perfected over a period of years. He smiled broadly and at the same time hardened his gaze and projected a silent message with all the conviction he could muster: *If you cross me up I'll tear your head right off your body.* The little man suddenly looked uncertain and backed further into the room.

"I got to be paid in advance," he said, trying to retain some advantage.

"Fair enough. I tell you what I'll do, Pop. I could use a few drinks to make up some of the sweat I lost, so here's an extra ten for a share in that bottle. How's that?" Massick took his billfold from his pocket, counted out thirty dollars and handed them over.

"Okay, I guess." The man took the money and, looking mollified, tucked it into his shirt pocket. "The whole bottle didn't cost ten."

"Consider it a reward for your hospitality to a weary traveller," Massick said jovially, smiling again. He was prepared to be generous while armed with the knowledge that when he left he would be taking the money back, along with any other cash and valuables his host happened to have around. "What's your name, Pop?"

"Ed. Ed Cromer."

"Nice to meet you, Ed." Massick went on into the room he had surveyed from the outside and picked up the whisky bottle from the table, observing as he did so that the small coloured objects his host had been packaging were dead butterflies and moths. "Is this some kind of a hobby you've got here?"

"Business," Cromer replied, squaring his thin shoulders importantly. "Profession."

"Is that a fact? Is there much demand for bugs?"

"Me and my partner supply lepidopterists – them's collectors – all over the state. All over the country."

"Your partner?" Massick slid his hand into the pocket containing the pistol and glanced towards the closed door of the bedroom. "Is he in there?"

"No!" The expression of pride vanished from Cromer's face and his eyes shuttled anxiously for a moment. "That's my private room in there. There's nobody allowed in there bar me."

Massick noted the reaction with mild interest. "There's no need to get uptight, Ed. It was just when you mentioned your partner . . ."

"He runs the store up in Tampa. Only comes down one day a month to pick up the new catch."

"He'll be here soon, will he?"

"Not for a couple of weeks. Say, mister, what's the third degree for? I mean, I could ask you who you are and where you're from and what you're doin' wanderin' around Big Cypress in the dark."

"That's right," Massick said comfortably. "You could ask."

He cleared some magazines from a wicker chair and sat down near the window, suddenly realizing how close he was to total exhaustion. His intention had been to press on towards the west coast in the morning, but unless Cromer had a swamp buggy parked out of sight nearby it might be best to wait until the partner arrived with transportation. It would be difficult to find a safer place to lie low and rest for a couple of weeks. Turning the matter over in his mind, he took off his sweat-stained jacket and draped it over the back of the chair, then settled back to drink whisky.

There followed fifteen minutes of almost total silence during which Cromer, who had returned to his meticulous sorting and mounting of butterflies, glanced expectantly at Massick each time he raised the bottle to his lips. At length, realizing there was going to be no taking of turns, he took a fresh bottle of Canadian Club from a cupboard in the corner and began drinking independently. After his initial querulousness he showed no sign of resenting his unexpected guest, but Massick noticed he was drinking somewhat faster than before and becoming less precise in his movements. Massick watched contentedly, enjoying his ability to cause apprehension in others simply by being near them, as Cromer fitted a jeweller's magnifier over his right eye and began examining a small heap of blue-winged insects one by one, using his flashlight to supplement the room's uncertain illumination.

"What are you doing now, Pop?" he said indulgently. "Is it all that hard to tell the boys from the girls?"

"Checkin' for look-alikes," Cromer mumbled. "Mimics, they're called. You don't know nothin' about mimics, do you?"

"Can't say I do."

Cromer sniffed to show his contempt. "Didn't think you would somehow. Even them so-called experts up in Jacksonville with their fancy college degrees don't know nothin' about mimics. *Nobody* knows more about mimics than I do, and one of these days . . ." He broke off, his narrow face taut with sudden belligerence, and took a long drink of whisky.

"You're going to show them a thing or two, are you, Professor?" Massick prompted. "Make them all sit up and take notice?"

Cromer glanced at the bedroom door, then selected two pale blue butterflies from the table and held them out on the palm of his hand. "Whaddaya say about them? Same or different?"

Massick eyed the closed door thoughtfully before turning his attention to the insects. "They look the same to me."

"Want to bet on it?"

"I'm not a gambling man."

"Just as well – you'da lost your money," Cromer said triumphantly. "This one on the left has a kinda blue glaze all over his wings and the birds leave him alone because he don't taste good. This other feller does taste good to birds, so he fools them by copyin' the same blue, but he does it by mixin' in blue bits and white bits on his wings. Of course, you need one of them microscopes to see it proper. I'm goin' to get me one of them microscopes real soon."

"Very interesting," Massick said, abstracted, noticing for the first time that the door to the room he had presumed to be a bedroom was secured by a farmhouse-type latch and that the latch was held down by a twist of wire. Was it possible, he wondered, that Cromer had something valuable hidden away? It was difficult to imagine what the shabby recluse might have, but it was a well-known fact that elderly people who lived in conditions of abject poverty often had large sums of money tucked into mattresses and under floorboards. In any case, there would be no harm in investigating the matter while he was actually on the premises. Deciding that no immediate action was required, he continued sipping whisky and pretending to listen to Cromer's rambling discourse on entomology.

The little man appeared to have an extensive though informal knowledge of his subject which he dispensed in an anecdotal folksy style, with frequent references to Seminole legends, but his words were becoming so slurred that it was almost impossible to follow his meaning at times. The practice of mimicry among insects, fish and animals seemed to fascinate him and he kept returning to it obsessively, drinking all the while, his face and clamped-down ears growing progressively redder as the level in his bottle went down.

"You ought to go easy on that stuff," Massick told him with some amusement. "I don't want to put you to bed."

"I can handle it." Cromer stood up, swaying even though he

was holding the edge of the table, and gazed at Massick with solemn blue eyes. "I gotta consult the head of the family."

He lurched to the outer door and disappeared through it into the night, already fumbling with his trouser zip. Massick waited a few seconds, stood up and was surprised to discover that he too was unsteady on his feet. He had forgotten that exhaustion and hunger would enhance the effects of the liquor he had consumed. Blinking to clear his vision, he crossed the room to the locked door, pulled the wire away from the latch and dropped it on the floor. He opened the door, took one step into the room beyond and froze in mid-stride, his jaw sagging in surprise.

There was a young woman lying on the narrow bed, her body covered by a single sheet.

At the sound of Massick's entrance she raised herself on one elbow – a strangely languid movement, as though she was weakened by illness – and he saw that she had smooth, swarthy skin and black hair. His impression that she was an Indian was strengthened by the fact that she had three dots tattooed in a triangle on her forehead, although he had never seen that particular marking before. She stared at him in silence for a moment, showing no signs of alarm, and began to smile. Her teeth were white, forming a flawless crescent.

"I'm sorry," Massick said. "I didn't know . . ." He backed out of the room, pulling the door closed, trying to understand why the sight of the woman had been so disconcerting. Was it the sheer unexpectedness of her presence in Cromer's bedroom? Was it that the circumstances suggested she was being held captive? Massick picked up his bottle, gulped some whisky and was wiping his mouth with the back of his hand when the answer to his questions stole quietly into his mind. She had looked at him – and had smiled.

He could not remember a single occasion in the twenty-odd years of his adult life on which a woman had set eyes on him for the first time and had reacted by smiling. As a youth he had spent hours before the mirror trying to decide what it was about his appearance that made all the girls in his age group avoid his eyes and refuse point blank to date him. There had been a two year period in which he had done his best to conform to the same image as the sexually successful young men in the neighbourhood – trying to put a twinkle into the slate pellets that were his eyes, trying to smile when every muscle in his face wanted to scowl, trying to crack jokes, to be lean-hipped, to be a good dancer – but the net result had been that the girls had shunned him more assiduously than before. After that he had simply begun taking them, whether they liked it or not. And none of them had liked it.

Over the years Massick had grown accustomed to the arrangement, so much so that he found real stimulation in the sudden look of mingled terror and disgust on a woman's face as she realised what was going to happen to her. Underneath it all, however, imprisoned far down in buried layers of his mind-body complex, there still lived a boyish Joe Massick who yearned for another kind of encounter, one in which there was gentleness in place of force, gladness in place of revulsion, in which soft arms welcomed as the world flowed out and away until there was nothing to see anywhere except eyes that shone with a special warm lustre and lips that smiled . . .

"That's better," Cromer said, coming in through the screen door. He went straight to his chair at the table, executed a lateral shuffle which showed he was quite drunk, and sat down before the assortment of insects and plastic boxes.

Massick returned to his own seat and gazed at Cromer with speculative eyes. Was it possible that the little man, in spite of his scrawny and dried-up appearance, had a taste for hot-blooded Indian girls? The notion inspired Massick with a sharp pang of jealousy. He had seen enough of the girl's body to know that she was strong-breasted, lush, ripe – and that she would be totally wasted on a miserable old stick like Cromer. If anybody was to bed down with her that night it ought to be Joe Massick, because he was the one who had been going through hell and needed relief from the tensions that racked his body, he was the one who had the size and strength to give the chick what she deserved, and because he was in that kind of a mood. Besides, she had smiled at him . . .

"The Calusas was the ones who knew this swamp," Cromer was muttering, staring down at a moth in its tiny crystal coffin. "They were here long before the Seminoles ever even *seen* the place, and they knew all about it, that's for sure . . . knew when the nymphs was turnin' into imagos . . . knew when it was time to pull up stakes and move on."

"You're a wily old bird, aren't you?" Massick said. "You've got this place stocked up with everything you need."

"Hear them cicadas out there?" Cromer, apparently unaware that Massick had spoken, nodded towards the black rectangle of the door. "Seventeen years they live under the ground, gettin' ready to come up and breed. It stands to reason there must be other critturs that takes longer – maybe thirty years, maybe fifty, maybe even a . . ."

"I'm a bit disappointed in you, Ed. I just didn't think you were the selfish type."

"Selfish?" Cromer, looking puzzled and hurt, attempted to focus his gaze on Massick. "What's this selfish?"

"You didn't introduce me to your friend."

"Friend? I got no . . ." Cromer's flushed, narrow face stiffened with consternation as he turned to look at the bedroom door. He threw himself forward on to his hands and knees, picked up the piece of wire Massick had discarded, and wrapped it around the latch, snorting with urgency as his clumsiness protracted an operation that should have been instantaneous.

Massick watched the performance with good humour. "Do you generally keep your lady friends locked up?"

"She . . . She's sick." Cromer got to his feet, breathing audibly, his eyes nervous and pleading. "Best left alone in there."

"She didn't look all that sick to me. What's her name?"

"Don't know her name. She wandered in here a couple of days ago. I'm lookin' after her, that's all."

Massick shook his head and grinned. "I don't believe you, Ed. I think you're a horny old goat and you're keeping that young piece in there for your own amusement. Shame on you!"

"You don't know what you're talkin' about. I tell you she's sick, and I'm looking after her."

Massick stood up, bottle in hand. "In that case we'll give her a drink – best medicine there is."

"No!" Cromer darted forward, grabbing for Massick's arm. "Listen, if you want to know the . . ."

Massick swung at him more out of irritation than malice, intending merely to sweep the little man out of his way, but Cromer seemed to fall on to his fist, magnifying the effect of the blow. The force of the impact returning along his forearm told Massick he had done some serious damage, and he stepped back. Cromer went down into a collision with the table, his eyes reduced to blind white crescents, and dropped to the floor with a slapping thud which could have been produced by a side of bacon. The sound alone was as good as a death certificate to Massick.

"You stupid old bastard," he whispered accusingly. He stared down at the body, adjusting to the new situation, then knelt and retrieved his money from Cromer's shirt pocket. A search of the dead man's personal effects yielded only a cheap wristwatch and eleven extra dollars in single bills. Massick put the watch and money away in his pocket. He took a firm grip on Cromer's collar, dragged the body to the screen door and out into the raucous darkness of the swamp. The chorus of insect calls seemed to grow louder as he moved away from the shanty, again creating the impression of an all-pervading sentience. In spite of the stifling heat Massick felt a crawling coldness between his shoulderblades. Suddenly appreciating the futility of trying to dispose of the body before daylight, he released his burden and groped his way back towards the sallow glimmers of the hurricane lamps.

Once inside the building, he bolted the outer door and went around the main room twitching curtains into place across the windows. As soon as he felt safe from the pressures of the watchful blackness he picked up the whisky bottle and drank from it until his throat closed against the rawness of the liquor. Somewhat restored by the alcohol, he allowed his thoughts to return to the bedroom door and there was a stirring of warmth low down in his belly as he remembered what lay beyond.

It's cosier this way, he thought. *Three always was a crowd.*

He put the bottle aside, went to the door and removed the wire from the latch. The door swung open easily, allowing a swath of light to fall across the bed, revealing that the black-haired girl was still lying down, apparently undisturbed by any commotion she may have heard. As before, she raised herself on one elbow to look up at him. Massick stood in the doorway and scanned her face, waiting for the change of expression to which he was so accustomed, the clouding of the eyes with fear and loathing, but – exactly as before – the girl began to smile. He bared his own teeth in a manufactured response, scarcely able to believe his luck.

"What's your name, honey?" he said, moving closer to the bed.

She went on smiling at him, her gaze locked into his, and there was nothing anywhere in her face to show that she had heard the question.

"Don't you have a name?" Massick persisted, a new idea beginning to form at the back of his mind. *Never had a deaf-mute before!*

The girl reacted by sitting up a little further, a movement which allowed the sheet to slip down from her breasts. They were the most perfectly formed that Massick had ever seen – rounded, almost pneumatic in their fullness, with upright nipples – and his mouth went dry as he advanced to the side of the bed and knelt down. The girl's dark eyes remained fixed on his, bold and yet tender, as he put out his hand and with his fingertips gently traced a line from the three dots on her forehead, down her cheek and neck and on to the smooth curvature of her breast. His hand lingered there briefly and was moving on towards the languorous upthrust of her hip – taking the edge of the sheet with it – when she made a small, inarticulate sound of protest and caught his wrist.

Thwarted and tantalised, Massick gripped the sheet with the intention of ripping it away from the lower part of her body, then he saw that the girl was still smiling. She let go of his wrists, raised her hands to his chest and began to undo his shirt, fumbling in her eagerness.

"You raunchy little so-and-so," Massick said in a gratified whisper. He got to his feet, tearing at his clothing and in a few seconds was standing naked beside the bed. The girl relaxed on to her pillow, waiting for him. He lowered his thick torso on to the bed beside her and brought his mouth down on hers. She returned his kiss in a curiously inexpert manner which served only to heighten his pleasure. Giving way to his impatience, he propped himself up on one elbow and used his free hand to throw back the sheet, his eyes hungering for the promised magical concourse of hip and belly and thigh unique to woman.

The ovipositor projecting from the she-creature's groin was a tapering, horny spike. Transparent eggs were already flowing from the aperture at its tip, bubbling and winking, sliming its sides, adding to the jellied mass of spawn which had gathered on her distended abdomen.

Massick had time for a single whimper of despair, then the she-creature was on him, bearing down with an inhuman strength which was scarcely necessary. The first probing stab from the ovipositor had hurt for only an instant, then ancient and merciful chemistries had taken over, obliterating all pain, inducing a flaccid paralysis which gripped his entire frame. He lay perfectly still, hushed and bemused, as his lover worked on him, stabbing again and again, skilfully avoiding vital organs, filling body cavities with the eggs which would soon produce a thousand hungry larvae.

It's a pity she had to change. I liked her better the other way – before those dots on her forehead changed into watchful black beads, before her eyes developed the facets and began to drift to the side of her head, before those magnificent breasts began reshaping themselves into a central pair of legs.

But she's kind to me, and that counts for a lot. Waits on me hand and foot, like an attentive lover. Even when I wake up during the night I can see her standing at the door of the room, always watching, always waiting.

But what's she waiting for? That's what I ask myself every so often, and when I do . . .

TO THE LETTER

Above Hillowen a tiny bell pinged a cracked F, reprising the note a moment later as he gently closed the door behind him. The basement room in which he found himself was divided by a tall counter of blackened wood, behind which were a bead-curtained door and shelves bearing rows of very old ledgers. The single window did not quite reach footpath level, and as a result the light which filtered into the room was tired and grey, the colour of January rain.

Whoever owns this place should apply for a grant to go Dickensian, Hillowen thought. *It doesn't look much like a threshold of earthly bliss, but I suppose it's best to stay shabby in this part of town if you don't want to attract too much attention.* He tapped on the counter, waited, then tapped more firmly.

The bead curtains chattered and from behind them came a small, elderly, dapper man with brown eyes and a pleasantly ugly face. He advanced with a friendly smile, placed his fingertips on the counter and gave a courteous little bow.

"Good afternoon to you, sir," he said in a voice which had no discernible accent and yet created the impression that English was not his first language. "May I be of assistance?"

"Mr Zurek?" Hillowen said.

The smile became faintly rueful. "For my sins."

"Ah, good! Well, my name is Hillowen and I'm a close friend of Mr George Lorrimer." Hillowen produced an airmail envelope from an inner pocket. "I have a letter of recommendation from him."

"Lorrimer," said Zurek, frowning slightly and showing no interest in the letter. "Lorrimer . . . Lorrimer . . ."

"You and he did a little business," Hillowen prompted.

"About six months ago. He's living abroad now," he added with a meaningful lowering of the voice.

"Ah, yes!" The brown eyes refocused on Hillowen. "Of course I remember the gentleman! I fixed him up somewhere in the South Seas, didn't I?"

"That's right – Tkumirui Island."

"With a selection of uninhibited maidens and the local copra concession."

"And permanent balmy weather!"

"That was it," Zurek said, chuckling. "A little banal, perhaps, but never mind . . . So long as he's happy, eh?"

"Oh, he's happy all right."

"Good, good!" Zurek's eyes had suddenly become less ingenuous than his smile. "And I take it, Mr Hillowen, that you are interested in a similar transaction?"

"Well . . ." Hillowen swallowed, suddenly feeling nervous now that the preliminaries were over. "Yes, that was the general idea."

"Hmmmm." Zurek's smile gradually faded, the brown eyes becoming professionally concerned. "Mr Hillowen, I know this will be a disappointment to you – especially after what you have heard from your friend – but I very much doubt that we can do business with you."

Hillowen stared at him, frowning. "Are you telling me you're not interested?"

"That's about it, I'm afraid."

"But this is *preposterous*!" Hillowen looked about him as if appealing to an invisible audience. "I thought you'd be coaxing me, wheedling, making all sorts of extravagant promises." His sense of grievance mounted rapidly. "After all, it's not Channel tunnel shares we're talking about – it's my immortal *soul*!"

"I know that, Mr Hillowen, and I'm sorry."

"But you were keen enough to do business with George only months ago! Surely one soul is just like another."

Zurek shook his head. "Mr Lorrimer is a young man with many years on earth ahead of him, and he has a regrettable tendency towards goodness. There was a very real possibility that, left to his own devices, he would have eventually acquired enough spiritual credits to cancel out the debits with which we all enter this world.

"The One I serve . . ." Zurek glanced around uneasily. "My principal felt that it was worthwhile inducing Mr Lorrimer to enter into a binding contract, whereas in your case, Mr Hillowen . . . Well, not to put too fine a point on it, you are practically in the bag."

"I'm not sure I like the sound of that," Hillowen said heatedly. "I haven't led a bad life. How do you know that I won't earn enough of these spiritual credits, as you call them, to get me into heaven?"

"That tie you're wearing – London School of Economics, isn't it?"

"Yes, but . . ."

Zurek patted his lips, a gesture which failed to conceal a smirk. "As I said, Mr Hillowen – you are practically in the bag."

"How can you be so sure I won't change?" Hillowen demanded. "I admit I'm no longer in the first flush of my youth, but I have quite a few years left in me yet. Time enough to get religion, time enough to . . ." He broke off as he saw that Zurek had pulled one of the ledgers from the shelves behind him and was opening it.

"Ah, yes," Zurek said, the index finger of his right hand coming to rest at an entry. "Norman Stanley Hillowen! You are fifty-three years of age and you have severe cardio-vascular problems, plus a liver which has absorbed far more than its fair share of punishment . . . Would you like to know *exactly* how much time you have left to you?"

"No!" Hillowen cowered back. "No man should ever be burdened with that kind of foreknowledge. Even a disciple of Satan himself would not reveal the exact figure."

"Four years," Zurek said unconcernedly. "Four years, all but . . . let me see . . . eleven days."

"This is terrible," Hillowen quavered. "You're not the sort of person I thought you were. When I came in here you seemed quite decent and pleasant, but now . . ."

"What did you expect?" Zurek cut in. "Use your brains, man! What do you think He would do to me if I didn't go all out to obtain the most advantageous terms for Him in every deal?"

"Deal?" Seizing on the word, Hillowen advanced to the counter on rubbery legs. "Did you say deal? Can I have a deal?"

"Are you sure you still want to do business?" Zurek squinted like a jeweller examining a watch. From behind him, a lean black cat sprang noiselessly on to the counter.

"With only four years left to me! For God's sake . . ." Hillowen paused as both Zurek and the cat shrank back from him. "I'm sorry . . . slip of the tongue . . . you must understand that all this has put me under a considerable strain."

"It's quite all right." Zurek was abstractedly stroking the cat.

"Thank you, thank you," Hillowen said fervently, leaning on the counter for support. "Now, here's what I propose. In exchange for my immortal soul . . ."

Zurek silenced him by raising his free hand. "Not so fast, Mr Hillowen! Before you go on, let me say at once that you cannot have material wealth. No currency notes, bankers' drafts or property deeds. No gold or other precious metals." As if quoting from a well-memorised legal document, he added, "No valuable stone, mineral or artefact, the last term to include products of genetic engineering and . . ."

"I don't care about any of those things," Hillowen cut in, "but – just as a matter of interest – why can't I have them?"

"Liquidity problems." Zurek gave a fatalistic shrug, then his smile began to revive. "However, for our more forward-looking clients, we can occasionally offer some quite interesting long-term securities."

Hillowen tilted his head pensively. "What kind of securities?"

"Well, if you wanted, I could probably get authorisation to offer you . . ." He gave a meditative sniff and tapped on the counter as though keying an invisible computer. "Let's say three thousand one-dollar preference shares in Kwangsi Imperial Railroads."

"Kwangsi? Where's that?"

"China."

"China!" cried Hillowen, his temples beginning to throb. "I don't give a toss about anything in China. What I really want is . . ."

"Another thing you can't have is extra time," Zurek said firmly, making it clear that he had no intention of relinquishing his superior bargaining position.

"There's no point in your asking for immortality, or even to live to be a hundred. Even if I were to make you a younger man again – say, in your forties – you would only go on for your allotted four more years and then something would happen to end your time on earth. Four years is the time remaining to you – and *nothing* can alter that."

Hillowen nodded. "I'm not as naïve as you seem to think. Four years may be a brief span of time, but if I am allowed to live them as I want to, those four years will contain enough ecstasy to make them equivalent to four *centuries*. I have had a good life, by the material standards which satisfy most people – an excellent house in Royal Tunbridge, respected position in the community, success in my profession, but the one thing denied to me, the one thing I craved above all others, was . . . was . . ."

"Political success is also out of the question," Zurek said quickly. "When I think of how we were taken in by that woman and what she has done . . ."

"No, no, *no*! I don't care about politics. All I want from what remains of my life is . . . is to be . . ."

"Say it, Mr Hillowen." Zurek picked the black cat up and cradled it against his chest. "Marge and I can be very understanding."

Hillowen took a deep breath and expelled it in a rush of words. "I want to be irresistible to women."

"Is *that* all?" Zurek said, unceremoniously dumping the cat on the floor. "Why didn't you say so at the start and save us a lot of time?"

"You mean . . . ?" Hillowen had to take a deep breath to ease the pounding in his chest. "You mean you'll do it?"

"Yes."

"But I mean *really* irresistible to women. I want them to go weak at the knees at the sight of me. I want them to be unable to keep their hands off me."

"I understand perfectly," Zurek said in matter-of-fact tones. "You are now totally irresistible to women – or you will be as soon as you sign the necessary contracts." He gave a doleful smile. "Nothing but forms these days, isn't it?"

Hillowen was taken aback and made suspicious – everything was now going almost too smoothly. "I must say you agreed to that very quickly."

"I'll let you into a little secret," Zurek said gently as he produced a sheaf of documents from under the counter. "You're the third irresistible-to-women I've had today."

Hillowen blushed and tried to look nonchalant. "Is it a perennial favourite?"

"Only among our male clients. Now, if you would like to read through these forms . . ."

"No, no," Hillowen said, still embarrassed. "I'm sure everything is fine. Mr Lorrimer tells me he is very happy with his contract. He says you are observing it to the letter."

"It's nice to know we're appreciated. In that case, if I could just have your signature here, please . . ."

"It doesn't have to be in blood, does it?" Hillowen peered uneasily at the proffered forms. "I've always been a bit squeamish . . ."

"Ballpoint will be fine," chuckled Zurek, taking a silver pen from his pocket. "Here, use mine. Now, if you will just sign here . . . that is . . . and once again here . . . and once more on the pink copy . . . and just once more for the computer centre . . . Fine!"

Ballpoint and contract vanished together, and Zurek shook Hillowen's hand with a smile of warmth and great sincerity. The cat leapt up on to the counter beside him and began to purr.

"Mr Hillowen," Zurek announced genially, "we have a deal!"

"Splendid," Hillowen said, his heart beginning to pound again. "So that's it, then, is it? I don't *feel* any different. What do I . . . ?"

"All you have to do, Mr Hillowen, is count to three."

"And as soon as I've done that I'll be . . . ."

"Completely," said Zurek, maintaining his smile.

"Well," Hillowen said, deciding not to waste a second more of his four years, "in that case – *one* . . ."

"Goodbye, Mr Hillowen."

"Goodbye," murmured Hillowen, and suddenly he was seeing everything through a kaleidoscope. Far from causing him alarm, the experience was quite amusing. Zurek's teeth, for example, had become a hinged circle of white; and the cat's head was a black billiard ball with sixteen ears.

"Two," Hillowen said, chuckling.

The kaleidoscope began to spin, and he gave himself up to a mild, delightful dizziness. The universe purred softly all around him. *Why is all this necessary?* he thought, but for some reason he was becoming very drowsy.

"Three," he whispered, and immediately was engulfed in a cosy darkness.

He awoke abruptly to sharp, random noises and found he was lying on his back, unable to see anything but meaningless patches of colour. The sounds were annoyingly loud, the colours intensely bright, and he had a vague impression of being in the open air.

Suddenly, from directly overhead, a blurred pink ovoid began to descend. He blinked at it uncertainly as it came into focus –and then, with a twinge of astonishment, he recognised it as a face. The face had melting blue eyes, a powdery nose, and a huge lipsticked mouth which was curving into a tender smile.

"Oooza booful boy, den?" it crooned. "Ooza booful, wooful ickle diddums?"

Wrinkling his tiny features, kicking with his tiny feet in rage and frustration, Hillowen threw his bright green rattle out of the pram. Then he began to howl.

COURAGEOUS NEW PLANET

The Savage was brooding in one brightly-lit corner of Foodroom 127, his shoulders hunched as he stared down at the smear-resistant surface of a table. A somaburger and a beaker of surrocoff remained untouched at his elbow. Once, apparently motivated by a dull curiosity, he squeezed some ketchup out of a plastic tomato on to the atomically polarised table-top, which naturally rejected the contamination. The red blob squirmed towards the edge like an agitated amoeba, dropped off into the Savage's lap and was promptly absorbed by the fabric of his 20th Century clothing. His lips moved silently, but only for a few seconds, then he returned to his apathetic reverie.

"I wonder why he isn't happy," Experimenter Gatesby said, watching the dejected figure through a discreet viewing device. "I mean, he would have *died* in that car accident if we hadn't snatched him forward to our time. You'd think he would be grateful."

"I raised the matter with him," replied Controller Carson. "All he said was, 'I'm a stranger in a strange land'. Apparently that's a quotation from the 20th Century writer Heinz-Lyon, author of a philosophical work called *57 Verities*."

Gatesby shook his head. "It's quite incredible. The Savage hasn't enjoyed one hour of sensuvision, and he won't even *look* at our best nymphobots. You know, it's going to affect our promotion prospects if we can't bring about a successful adjustment."

"We'd better talk to him again," Carson said. He turned to the nearest dispensomat and keyed in the specification for a capsule which would increase his persuasiveness, psychic aura and problem-solving ability. A bright plastic egg dropped into his hand a second later. Carson popped it into his mouth and, thus fortified, set off with springy gait for another meeting with the Savage. Gatesby, who had declined a capsule, trailed a short distance behind.

"Frankly, I don't understand you," Carson said. "We've brought you forward in time to a world in which disease, hunger and war have been abolished. There is no need for anyone to work, unless he wishes to, and every citizen can command greater sensual gratification than was available to the most powerful kings of old. This is the future the people of your era could only dream of – and yet you are not happy. Why? Please tell me why."

"If you must know," the Savage said, twiddling with his beard, "it's partly because I was a science fiction fan."

Carson turned in the direction of his colleague and raised a questioning eyebrow.

"I ran a check on the term the first time he used it," Gatesby said. "Apparently he was a devotee of a small group of scientific visionary writers with names like Azimuth, Anny Logg, and Funnygut. Those writers spent most of their time trying to visualise the future. They didn't all have strange names, though – one of the best was called Shaw."

The Savage stirred and his eyes glowed momentarily. "Ah, yes – Shaw!"

"But that explains nothing," Carson protested. "In fact, it makes things more baffling. If you were so intrigued by the future you should be overjoyed at finding yourself actually in it. Why aren't you deliriously happy?"

"Why? *Why*?" The Savage straightened up, his face registering an interplay of emotions – anger, despair, contempt. "Don't you see – you slithy tove, you miserable greep-crottler – that here there is too much of everything? There's none of the variety and challenge, longing and disappointment that add spice to life. You live in an endless desert of plentitude, a desert from which there is no escape."

"Escape?"

"That's what I said. I loved science fiction because it allowed me to burst through the gloomy barricades of the 20th Century –

it was a dapple of primary colour on the dark palette of the times. The human soul feeds on contrast. Pleasure has to be tempered with pain, love with hate . . ."

"But a nymphobot can be instructed to inflict pain," Carson said quickly. "Within certain . . . ."

". . . pre-set limits," the Savage sneered. "But is there any chance that one of your fluid-solenoid automata would try to kill me through jealousy of one of her mass-produced sisters? No, this perfect plastic world of yours has been rendered germ-free, sterilised, regardless of the fact that life itself is a coloured stain on the white radiance of eternity. Everything that made us human has been cauterised out of existence.

"Oh God, how I miss those things – the unpredictability of a real woman, the ever-varying taste of a living ale, the hiss and kiss of rain, the choking smell of a pensioner's black tobacco, the irrationality of religion and politics, even the barely-suppressed violence of a football crowd, and . . ."

"Just a minute," Carson cut in. "Did you say football? Do you like soccer?"

"Next to the science fiction works of Captain S. P. Meek, there was nothing I loved more," the Savage breathed. "But of course all that will have been swept away by what you call progress."

Carson shook his head. "No, it hasn't – soccer is our most popular sport."

"What?" The Savage gazed from one man to the other, jaw sagging, then his brow cleared. "Oh, I understand – you have reduced it to mere electronic blobs on the face of a cathode ray tube."

"But that would have destroyed the essence of the game." Carson gave the Savage a reassuring smile. "Soccer is, and always will be, a contact sport – a test of human strength, speed and skill."

"You mean . . . ?"

"I mean that league football is alive and thriving in 25th Century Britain," Carson said. "Would it cheer you up if we were to attend tomorrow night's big match here in London? I'm sure that even in your time Arsenal and Manchester City were serious contenders for the F.A. cup."

"Arsenal and City in a cup match!" The Savage lowered his head, but not before Carson and Gatesby had glimpsed the welling of his tears. They exchanged triumphant glances, then stood up and diplomatically left the Savage to the quietness of his room.

The atmosphere of a big match had not changed much in five centuries – and yet the Savage seemed oddly dissatisfied.

He paced uneasily in the directors' box, staring down at the floodlit turf, the patterned movements of the twenty-two players, the rippling of the rapt multitudes on the terraces. Several minutes of the match's first half ticked by, with the Savage growing more and more agitated, then he came to an abrupt halt. A frown gathered on his bearded countenance as he surveyed the packed ground below.

Gatesby, who had been observing him with some disquiet, said, "Is not everything to your liking?"

"The crowd is so orderly . . . so passive . . ." The Savage turned to Gatesby with a look of accusation. "I see only Arsenal scarves down there. Those are *all* Arsenal supporters."

"Naturally."

"But where is the opposition? Where are the Manchester City supporters?"

"In Manchester, of course. They're watching the match in Manchester."

"Huh!" The Savage looked disgusted. "On television!"

Gatesby shook his head emphatically. "Not at all! Everybody accepts that television cannot convey the real atmosphere of a soccer match – one has to be there in person. In Manchester they are watching the actual match – just as we are doing here."

The Savage clenched his fists in annoyance. "What kind of double-talk is this? Either we are watching the real match or . . ."

"Perhaps I should put in a word here," said Controller Carson smoothly. "You see, by the end of the 20th Century the social problems associated with soccer hooliganism had grown so great –

with entire districts being destroyed by visiting supporters on the rampage – that it looked as though football would have to be suppressed altogether. Then, happily, science came to the rescue. Thanks to the great progress made in robotics it became possible to eliminate the whole concept of the 'away' match. Every soccer game is now a 'home' match, and the crowds of proles are easy to control while at their own local ground."

"Robotics?" The Savage glanced suspiciously at the weaving figures on the floodlit pitch. "Are you telling me that is a contest between two teams of robots?"

Carson laughed aloud. "Of course not! That would be a poor substitute indeed for the traditional clash between two teams of red-blooded men."

"But . . ."

"Don't you see it? *One* team out there, the visiting team, is composed of robots – each of them perfectly linked to and controlled by a human counterpart up in Manchester. Similarly, every one of our human Arsenal players out there is linked to a robot counterpart which was sent up to Manchester this morning. Every movement of every human player is faithfully duplicated at the other venue, every spin and slice of the ball is replicated to perfection. In this way the same match can be played in two different places, in front of two crowds of *home* supporters – thus eliminating the old problem of hooliganism at away matches."

"But this is all wrong," the Savage cried. "That's why the match is so *dead*. The human players aren't being fired and inspired and driven by the emotional energies generated in the crowd. All the sense of tribal conflict is gone from the terraces, the catharsis of personal involvement is missing, the hint of danger . . ."

"Wait a minute! Why did the soccer-supporting public accept this terrible new system so meekly and passively? Why didn't some of them insist on travelling to away matches just as they always did?"

Carson put a capsule into his mouth and swallowed it. "Some of them did at first, then the Government realised it was in the best interests of everybody in the country to limit the mobility of proles. A geosynchronous satellite blankets the country with a type of radiation which, unless a person is specially protected, induces pain and severe nausea in all who travel through it laterally for more than about five kilometres. In a way, it almost makes the dual match idea redundant, except that players have got used to never having to waste time travelling in person, and never having to face a hostile foreign crowd in person. The whole system is very effective."

"It's evil and inhuman," the Savage whispered, his eyes smouldering in a face which had become a brooding mask. "Tell me, my good friends, am *I* protected from your cursed radiation which keeps ordinary men in invisible cages?"

"There is no restriction on your mobility," Gatesby said, "but I don't see . . ."

"You will – I promise you." The Savage strode to the edge of the directors' box, and in one powerful flowing movement vaulted the balustrade and disappeared into the milling crowds below. At that moment one of the players on the lime-glowing turf scored a goal and the stadium echoed with polite orderly applause.

"What are we going to do?" Gatesby said when the cheering had subsided. "Should we inform the police?"

"Don't bother," Carson replied comfortably. "I was getting pretty bored with the Savage – and he will soon learn that there is absolutely nothing he can do to upset the system."

Controller Carson had cause to remember his words when, only a month later at the F.A. cup final, he was struck on the head by a beer bottle which had been launched with superhuman accuracy from the hand of a robot soccer hooligan, part of a gang which – under the leadership of a wild-eyed and bearded figure – had begun kicking up a very human kind of hell on terraces throughout the length and breadth of the country.

CUTTING DOWN

Herley was awakened by the sounds of his wife getting out of bed. Afraid of seeing her nude body, he kept his eyes closed and listened intently as she padded about the room. There came a silky electrostatic crackling as she removed her nightdress – at which point he squeezed his eyes even more tightly shut – then a rustling of heavier material which told him she had donned a dressing gown. He relaxed and allowed the morning sun to penetrate his lashes with bright oily needles of light.

"What would you like for breakfast?" June Herley said.

He still avoided looking at her. "I'll have the usual – coffee and a cigarette." *That isn't enough*, he added mentally. *Breakfast is the most important meal of the day.*

She paused at the bedroom door. "That isn't enough. Breakfast is the most important meal of the day."

"All right then – coffee and *two* cigarettes."

"Oh, *you!*" She went out on to the landing and he heard her wallowing progress all the way down the stairs and into the kitchen. Herley did not get up immediately. He cupped his hands behind his head and once again tried to fathom the mystery of what had happened to the girl he had married. It had taken a mere eight years for her to change from a slim vivacious creature into a hopeless, sagging hulk. In that time the flat cones of her breasts had become vast sloping udders, and the formerly boyish buttocks and thighs had turned into puckered sacks of fat which at the slightest knock developed multi-hued bruises which could persist for weeks. For the most part her face was that of a stranger, but there were times when he could discern the features of that other June, the one he had loved, impassively drowning beneath billows of pale tissue.

It was, he sometimes thought, the mental changes which

frightened, sickened, baffled and enraged him the most. The other June would have endured any privation to escape from the tallowy prison of flesh, but the woman with whom he now shared his home blandly accepted her condition, aiding and abetting the tyrant of her stomach. Her latest self-deception – which was why she had begun to fuss about breakfast – was a diet which consisted entirely of protein and fat, to be eaten in any quantity desired as long as not the slightest amount of carbohydrate was consumed. Herley had no idea whether or not the system would work for other people, but he knew it had no chance in June's case. She used it as a justification for eating large greasy meals three or four times a day in his presence, and in between times – in his absence – filling up on sweetstuffs.

The aroma of frying ham filtering upwards from the kitchen was a reminder to Herley that his wife had yet to admit her new form of dishonesty. He got up and strode swiftly to the landing and down the stairs, moving silently in his bare feet, and opened the kitchen door. June was leaning over the opened pedal-bin and eating chocolate ice cream from a plastic tub. On seeing him she gave a startled whimper and dropped the tub into the bin.

"It was almost empty," she said. "I was only . . ."

"It's all right – you're not committing any crime," he said, smiling. "My God, what sort of a life would it be if you couldn't enjoy your food?"

"I thought you . . ." June gazed at him, relieved but uncertain. "You must hate me for being like this."

"Nonsense!" Herley put his arms around his wife and drew her to him, appalled as always by the *looseness* of her flesh, the feeling that she was wrapped in a grotesque and ill-fitting garment. In his mid-thirties, he was tall and lean, with a bone structure and sparse musculature which could be seen with da Vincian clarity beneath taut dry skin. Watching the gradual invasion of June's body by adipose tissue had filled him with such a dread of a similar fate that he lived on a strictly fat-free diet and often took only one meal a day. In addition he exercised strenuously at least three times a week, determined to burn off every single oily molecule that might have insinuated itself into his system.

"I'll have my coffee as soon as it's ready," he said when he judged he had endured the bodily contact long enough. "I have to leave in thirty minutes."

"But this is your day off."

"Special story. I've got an interview lined up with Hamish Corcoran."

"Why couldn't it have been on a working day?"

"I was lucky to get him at all – he's practically a recluse since he quit the hospital."

"I know, poor man," June said reflectively. "They say the shock of what happened to his wife drove him out of his mind."

"They say lots of things that aren't worth listening to." Herley had no interest in the biochemist's personal life, only in a fascinating aspect of his work about which he had heard for the first time a few nights earlier.

"Don't be so callous," June scolded. "I suppose if you came home and found that some psycho had butchered me you'd just shrug it off and go out looking for another woman."

"Not until after the funeral." Herley laughed aloud at his wife's expression. "Don't be silly, dear – you know I'd never put anybody in your place. Marriage is a once and for all thing with me."

"I should hope so."

Herley completed his morning toilet, taking pleasure in stropping his open-bladed razor and shaving his flat-planed face to a shiny pinkness. He had a cup of black coffee for breakfast and left June still seated in the kitchen, the slabs of her hips overflowing her chair. She was lingering at the table with obvious intent, in spite of already having consumed enough calories to last the day. *There's no point in getting angry about it*, Herley thought. *Especially not today . . .*

He walked the mile to Aldersley station at a brisk pace, determined not to miss the early train to London. Hamish Corcoran had lived in Aldersley during his term at the hospital, but on retiring he had moved to a village near Reading, some sixty miles away on the far side of London, and reaching him was going to take a substantial part of the day. The journey was likely to be tiresome, but Herley had a feeling it was going to be worth his while. As a sub-editor on the *Aldersley Post* he liked to supplement his income by turning in an occasional feature article written in his own time. Normally he would not have considered travelling more than a few miles on research – his leisure hours were too precious – but this was not a normal occasion, and the rewards promised to be greater than money.

As he had feared, the train and bus connections were bad, and it was nearly midday by the time he located the avenue of mature beeches and sun-splashed lawns in which Corcoran lived. Corcoran's was a classical turn-of-the-century, double-fronted house which was all but hidden from the road by banks of shrubbery. Herley felt a twinge of envy as he walked up the gravel drive – it appeared that becoming too eccentric to continue in employment, as Corcoran was reputed to have done, had not seriously affected his standard of living.

He rang the bell and waited, half-expecting the door to be opened by a housekeeper, but the grey-haired man who appeared was undoubtedly the owner. Hamish Corcoran was about sixty, round-shouldered and slight of build, with a narrow face in which gleamed humorous blue eyes and very white dentures. In spite of the summertime warmth he was wearing a heavy cardigan and a small woollen scarf, beneath which could be seen a starched collar and a blue bow tie.

"Hello, Mr Corcoran," Herley said. "I phoned you yesterday. I'm Brian Herley, from the *Post*."

Corcoran gave him a fluorescent smile. "Come in, my boy, come in! It's very flattering that your editor should want to publish something about my work."

Herley decided against mentioning that nobody in the editorial office knew of his visit. "Well, the *Post* has always been interested in the research work at Aldersley, and we think the public should know more about its achievements."

"Quite right! Now, if you're anything like all the other gentlemen of the Press I've met you're not averse to a drop of malt. Is that right?"

"It *is* a rather thirsty sort of a day." Herley followed the older

man into a cool brown room at the rear of the house and was
installed in a leather armchair. He examined the room, while
Corcoran was pouring drinks at a sideboard, and saw that the
shelves which lined the walls were occupied by a jumble of
books, official-looking reports and odd items of electronic
equipment whose function was not apparent. Corcoran handed
him a generous measure of whisky in a heavy crystal tumbler and
sat down at the other side of a carved desk.

"And how are things in Aldersley?" Corcoran said, sipping his
drink.

"Oh, much the same as ever."

"In other words, not worth talking about – especially after
you've come such a long way to interview me." Corcoran took
another sip of whisky and it dawned on Herley that the little man
was quite drunk.

"I've got lots of time, Mr Corcoran. Perhaps you could give me
a general rundown, in layman's terms, on this whole business of
slow muscles and fast muscles. I must confess I've never really
understood what it was all about."

Corcoran looked gratified and immediately plunged into a
moderately technical discourse on his work on nerve chemistry,
speaking with the eager fluency of one who has for a long time
been deprived of an audience. Herley pretended to be interested, even making written notes from time to time, waiting for the
opportunity to discuss the real reason for his visit. He already
knew that the research unit at Aldersley General had been
involved in discoveries concerning the basic structure of muscle
tissue. Experiments had shown that "fast" muscles such as those
of the leg could be changed into "slow" muscles – like those of the
abdomen – simply by severing the main nerves and reconnecting
them to the wrong set, in a process analagous to reversing the
leads from a battery.

The implication had been that the type of muscle was
determined, not by a genetic blueprint, but by some factor in the
incoming nerve impulses. Hamish Corcoran had come up with a
theory that the phenomenon was caused by a trophic chemical
which trickled from nerve to muscle. He had already begun work

on identifying and isolating the chemical involved when the tragedy of his wife's death had interrupted his researches. Soon afterwards he had been persuaded to retire. The rumour which had circulated in Aldersley was that he had gone mad, but no details had ever become public, thanks to a vigorous covering-up job by a hospital which had no wish to see its reputation endangered.

"I was quite wrong about the chemical nature of the nerve influence," Corcoran was saying. "It has since been established that electrical stimulus is the big factor – slow muscles receive a fairly continuous low-frequency signal, fast muscles receive brief bursts at a much higher frequency – but the fascinating thing about the science game is the way in which one's mistakes can be so valuable. You can set off for China, so to speak, and discover America. In my case, America was a drug which offered complete and effortless control of obesity."

The final statement alerted Herley like a plunge into cold water.

"That's rather interesting," he said. "Control of obesity, eh? I would have thought there was a huge commercial potential there."

"You would have thought wrong, my boy."

"Oh? Do you mean it wasn't possible to manufacture the drug?"

"Nothing of the sort! I was able to produce a pilot batch with very little difficulty." Corcoran glanced towards a bookshelf on his right, then noticed that his glass was empty. He stood up and went to the sideboard, for the third time during the interview, to pour himself a fresh drink. Herley took the opportunity to scan the shelf which had drawn the older man's gaze and his attention was caught by a small red box. It was heavily ornamented and cheap-looking, the sort of thing that was turned out in quantity for the foreign souvenir market, and seemed more than a little out of place in its surroundings.

That's where the pills are, Herley thought, savagely triumphant. Until that moment he had suffered from lingering doubts about the information he had received from a drunken laboratory technician a few nights earlier. He had been talking to the technician in a bar, half-heartedly following up a lead about administrative malpractice in the hospital, when the tip of the story about Corcoran's secret wonder-drug had surfaced through a sea of irrelevancies. It had cost Herley quite a bit of money to obtain what little information he had, and he also had been forced to acknowledge the possibility that – as sometimes happens to newsmen – he had been skilfully conned. Until the moment when Corcoran had glanced at the red box . . .

"Why aren't you drinking, young man?" Corcoran said with mock peevishness, returning to his desk. His voice was still crisp and clear, but triangles of crimson had appeared on his cheeks and his gait was noticeably unsteady.

Herley took a miniature sip of his original drink, barely wetting his lips. "One is enough for me on an empty stomach."

"Ah, yes." Corcoran ran his gaze over Herley's lean frame. "You don't eat much, do you?"

"Not a lot. I like to control my weight."

Corcoran nodded. "Very wise. Much better than letting your weight control you."

"There's no chance of that." Herley laughed comfortably.

"It's no laughing matter, my boy," Corcoran said. "I'm speaking quite literally – when the adipose tissue in a person's body achieves a certain threshold mass it can, *quite literally*, begin to govern that person's actions. It can take over that person's entire life."

For the first time in the interview Herley detected a trace of irrationality in his host's words, the first confirmation of the old rumours of eccentricity. Corcoran seemed to be talking fancifully, at the very least, and yet something in what he was saying was generating a strange disturbance in Herley's mind. How many times had he asked himself why it was that June, once so meticulous about her appearance, now allowed herself to be dominated by her appetite?

"Some people are a bit short on will-power," he said. "They get into the habit of over-eating."

"Do you really believe that's all there is to it? Doesn't that strike you as being very strange?"

"Well, I . . ."

"Consider the case of a young woman who has become grossly overweight," Corcoran cut in, speaking very quickly and with an azure intensity in his eyes. "I chose the example of a woman because women traditionally place greater value on physical acceptability. Consider the case of a young woman who is say fifty per cent or more above her proper weight. She is ugly, pathetic, *ill*. She is either socially ostracised or elects to cut herself off from social contact. Her chances of sexual fulfilment are almost zero, her life expectancy is greatly reduced, and the years she can anticipate promise nothing but sickness and self-disgust and unhappiness. Do you get the picture?"

"Yes." Herley moved uneasily in his chair.

"Now we come to the truly significant aspect of the case, and it is this. That woman *knows* that her suffering is unnecessary, that she can escape from her torment, that she can transform her physical appearance. She can become slim, healthy, attractive, energetic. She can avail herself of all that life has to offer. There's very little to it – all she has to do is eat a normal diet. It's a ridiculously trivial price to pay, the greatest bargain of all time – like being offered a million pounds for your cast-off socks – but what happens?" Corcoran paused to take a drink and the glass chittered momentarily against his teeth.

"Actually, I've seen what happens," Herley said, wondering where the discourse was leading. "She goes right on eating more than her body needs."

Corcoran shook his head. "That's the orthodox and simplistic view, my boy. She goes on eating more than she, as the original person, needs – but, in fact, she is eating exactly the right amount to suit the needs of the adipose organ."

Herley's uneasiness increased. "I'm sorry. I'm afraid I don't quite . . ."

"I'm talking about fat," Corcoran said fervently. "What do you know about fat?"

"Well . . . what is there to know about it? Isn't it just like lard?"

"A common misconception. Human body fat is actually a very complex substance which acts like a very large organ. Most people think of the adipose organ as having a poor blood supply, probably because it's pale and bleeds little during surgery, but in fact it has a very extensive blood supply in very small capillaries, and the density of those capillaries is greater than in muscle, second only to liver. More important, the adipose organ also has a subtle network of nerves which are locked into the central nervous system and capable of reacting with it."

Corcoran took another drink, eyeing Herley over the rim of the glass. "Do you understand what I'm saying?"

"No." Herley gave an uncertain laugh. "Not really."

Corcoran leaned forward, red pennants flaring on his cheeks. "I'm telling you that the adipose organ has a life of its own. It behaves like any other successful parasite – selfishly, looking out for its own interests. It controls its own environment as best it can, which means that it controls its host. That's why obese people have the compulsion to go on over-eating, to go on being fat – no adipose organ willingly allows itself to be killed!"

Herley stared back at the older man with real anxiety in his heart. He had always had a phobia about insanity, and now he was experiencing a powerful urge to flee.

"That's a very . . . interesting theory," he said, draining his glass to banish the sudden dryness of his mouth.

"It's more than a theory," Corcoran replied. "And it explains why a person who tries to slim down finds it harder and harder to keep to a diet – when the adipose organ feels threatened it fights more strongly for its life. A person who loses *some* adipose tissue almost always puts it back on again. It's only in the very rare cases where the determined slimmer manages to starve the adipose organ down below its threshold mass for autonomous consciousness that he successfully normalises his weight. Then dieting suddenly becomes easy, and he tends to remain slim for life."

Herley did his best to appear unruffled. "This is really fascinating, but I don't see how it tallies with what you said earlier. Surely, if it were possible to produce a drug that would effectively . . . ah . . . kill this . . . ah . . . adipose organ it would have tremendous commercial potential."

"The drug *can* be manufactured," Corcoran said, again glancing to the right. "I told you I had produced a pilot batch, in the form of a targeted liposome. For a human adult, four 1 c.c. doses at daily intervals is enough to guarantee permanent normalisation of body weight."

"Then what's the problem?"

"Why, the adipose organ itself," Corcoran said with an indulgent smile. "It fights very effectively against a slow death – so how do you imagine it would react to the prospect of a sudden death? Without understanding what was happening inside his own body and nervous system the patient would feel a powerful aversion to the use of the drug and would go to any lengths to avoid it. I think that takes care of your commercial potential."

This is getting crazier and crazier, Herley thought.

"What if you disguised the drug?" he said. "Or what if it was administered by force?"

"I don't think the adipose organ would be deceived, especially after the first dose – and there *is* such a thing as the medical ethic."

Herley stared at Corcoran's flushed countenance, wondering what to do next. It was easy to see why Aldersley General had decided to part company with Corcoran on the quiet. Although a brilliant pioneer in his field, the man was obviously deranged. Had it not been for the independent evidence from the laboratory technician, Herley would have had severe doubts about the efficiency of Corcoran's radical new drug. Now the substance seemed less attainable and therefore more desirable than ever.

"If that's the case," Herley said tentatively, "I don't suppose you'd ever be interested in selling the pilot batch?"

"*Sell* it!" Corcoran gave a wheezing laugh. "Not for a million pounds, my boy. Not for a billion."

"I have to admire your principles, sir – I'm afraid I'd be tempted by a few hundred," Herley said with a rueful grimace, getting to his feet and dropping his notebook into his pocket.

"It's been a pleasure talking to you, but I have to get back to Aldersley now."

"It's been more of a pleasure for me – I get very bored living in this big house all by myself since my . . ." Corcoran stood up and shook Herley's hand across his desk. "Don't forget to let me have a copy."

"A copy? Oh, yes. I'll send you half-a-dozen when the article is printed." Herley paused and looked beyond Corcoran towards the garden which lay outside the room's bay window. "That's a handsome shrub, isn't it? The one with the grey leaves."

Corcoran turned to look through the window. "Ah, yes. My *Olearia scilloniensis*. It does very well in this soil."

Herley, moving with panicky speed, side-stepped to the bookshelves on his left, snatched the red box from its resting place and slipped it inside his jacket, holding it between his arm and ribcage. He was back in his original position when Corcoran left the window and came to usher him out of his room. Corcoran steadied himself by touching his desk as he passed it.

"Thanks again," Herley said, trying to sound casual in spite of the hammering of his heart. "Don't bother coming to the front door with me – I can see myself out."

"I'm sure you can, but there's just one thing before you go."

Herley drew his lips into a stiff smile. "What's that, Mr Corcoran?"

"I want my belongings back." Corcoran extended one hand. "The box you took from the shelf – I want it back. *Now!*"

"I don't know what you're talking about," Herley said, trying to sound both surprised and offended. "If you're suggesting . . ."

He broke off, genuinely surprised this time, as Corcoran lunged forward and tried to plunge his hands inside his jacket. Herley blocked the move, striving to push Corcoran away from him and being thwarted by the little man's unexpected strength and tenacity. The two men revolved in an absurd shuffling dance, then Herley's superior power manifested itself with an abrupt breaking of Corcoran's hold. Corcoran was forcibly propelled backwards for the distance of one pace and was jolted to a halt by the edge of the marble fireplace, which caught him at the base of the skull. His eyes turned upwards on the instant, blind crescents of white, and blood spurted from his nose. He dropped into the hearth amid an appalling clatter of fire irons, and lay very, very still.

"You did that yourself," Herley accused, backing away, mumbling through the fingers he had pressed to his lips. "That's what you get for drinking too much. That's . . ."

He stopped speaking and, driven by a pounding sense of urgency, looked around the room for evidence of his visit. The whisky tumbler he had used was still sitting on the arm of the leather chair. He picked it up in trembling fingers, dried and polished it with his handkerchief and placed it among others on the sideboard, then went to the desk. Among the papers scattered on its surface he found a large business diary which was open at the current date. He examined the relevant page, making sure there was no note of his appointment, then hurried out of the room without looking at the obscene object in the hearth.

Herley felt an obscure and dull surprise on discovering that the world outside the house was exactly as he had left it – warm and green, placidly summery, unconcerned. Even the patterns of sunlight and leafy shadow looked the same, as though the terrible event in Corcoran's study had taken place in another continuum where time did not exist.

Grateful for the screening effect of the trees and tall shrubs, Herley tightened his grip on the red box and started out for home.

"It's wonderful," June breathed, unable to divert her gaze from the small bottle which Herley had set on the kitchen table. "It seems too good to be true."

"But it *is* true – I guarantee it." Herley picked up the hypodermic syringe he had found in the red box and examined its tip. He had made important decisions on the journey back from Reading. His wife already knew where he had been during the day, so there was nothing for it but to wait until the news of Corcoran's "accidental" death came out and utter appropriate words. If the body was found quickly: *Good God! It must have happened to the poor man soon after I left him – but I don't think there's any point in my getting mixed up in an inquest, do you?* If, as was quite possible, there was a lengthy delay before the corpse came to light: *Fancy that! I wonder if it could have happened around the time I went to see him . . .*

In either case, to prevent June talking about it and perhaps forging links in other people's minds, he was going to lie about where and how he had obtained the drug.

"Just think, darling," he said enthusiastically. "Four little shots is all it will take. No dieting, no boring counting of calories, no trouble. I promise you, you're going to be your old self again."

June glanced down at her squab-like breasts and the massive curvature of her stomach which the loosest fitting dress was unable to disguise. "It would be wonderful to wear nice clothes again."

"We'll get you a wardrobe full of them. Dresses, undies, swimsuits – the lot."

She gave a delighted laugh. "Do you really think I could go on the beach again?"

"You're *going*, dear – in a black bikini."

"Mmm! I can't wait."

"Neither can I." Herley opened the small bottle, inverted it and filled the hypodermic with colourless fluid. He had been disappointed to discover that the drug was not in tablet form, which he could have slipped unannounced into June's food, but there was nothing he could do to alter the situation. It was fortunate, he realised, that he knew how to use a needle.

"I don't think we need bother about sterilising swabs and all that stuff," he said. "Give me your arm, dear."

June's eyes locked with his and her expression became oddly wary. "Now?"

"What do you mean now? Of course it's now. Give me your arm."

"But it's so soon. I need time to think."

"About what?" Herley demanded. "You don't think I'm planning to poison you, I hope."

"I . . . I don't even know where that stuff came from."

"It's from one of the best Harley Street clinics, June. It's something brand new, and it cost me a fortune."

June's lips had begun to look bloodless. "Well, why doesn't the doctor give me the injections himself?"

"For an extra hundred guineas? Talk sense!"

"I am talking sense – giving injections is a skilled job."

"You saw me giving dozens of them to your mother."

"Yes," June said heatedly. "And my mother died."

Herley gaped at her, unable to accept what he had heard. "June! Is that remark supposed to contain any kind of logic? It was *because* your mother was dying that she was on morphine."

"I don't care." June turned her back on him and walked towards the refrigerator, the great slabs of her hips working beneath the flowered material of her dress. "I'm not going to be rushed into anything."

Herley looked from her to the syringe in his hand and blood thundered in his ears. He hit her with the left side of his body, throwing her against the refrigerator and pinning her there while his left arm clamped around her neck. She heaved against him convulsively, once, then froze into immobility as the needle ran deep into the hanging flesh of her upper right arm. Herley was reminded of some wild creature which was genetically conditioned to yield at the moment of being taken by a predator, but the pang of guilt he felt served only to increase his anger. He drove a roughly estimated cubic centimetre of the fluid into his wife's bloodstream, withdrew the needle and stepped back, his breath coming in a series of low growls which he was unable to suppress.

June clamped her left hand over the bright red lentil which had appeared on her arm, and turned to face him. "Did I deserve that, Brian?" she said sadly and gently. "Do I really deserve that sort of treatment?"

"Don't try your old Saint June act on me," he snapped. "It used to work, but things are going to be different from now on."

A fine rain began to fall in mid-evening, denying Herley the solace of working in the garden. He sat near the window in the front room, pretending to read a book and covertly watching June as she whiled away the hours before bed. She maintained a wounded silence, staring at the dried flower arrangement which screened the unused fireplace. At intervals of fifteen minutes she went foraging in the kitchen, and on her returns made no attempt to hide the fact that she was chewing. Once she brought back an economy-size container of salted peanuts and steadily munched her way through them, filling the whole room with the choking smell of peanut oil and saliva.

Herley endured the performance without comment, his mood a strange blend of boredom and terror. Slipping away from Corcoran's house could have been, he saw in retrospect, a serious blunder. It might have been better to telephone the police immediately and present them with a perfectly credible, unimpeachable story about Corcoran getting drunk and falling backwards against the mantlepiece. That way he could have kept the drug, hiding it in his pocket, and emerged from the affair free and clear. As it was, he was going to have some difficult explaining to do should the authorities manage to connect him with Corcoran's death.

Why couldn't the little swine have been reasonable? Herley repeated the question to himself many times during the dismal suburban evening and always arrived at the same answer. Anybody who was crazy enough to regard subcutaneous fat, simple disgusting blubber, as having sentience and a pseudo-life of its own was hardly likely to listen to reason in any other respect. The very idea was enough to give Herley a cold, crawling sensation along his spine, adding a hint of Karloffian horror to the evening's natural gloom.

As the rain continued the air in the house steadily grew cooler and more humid, beginning to smell of toadstools, and Herley wished he had lit the fire hours earlier. He also found himself longing, uncharacteristically, for an alcoholic drink – regardless of the empty calories it would have represented – but there was nothing in the house. He contented himself by smoking cigarette after cigarette.

At 11.30 he stood up and said, "I think that's enough hilarity for one evening – are you going to bed?"

"Bed?" June looked up at him, seemingly without understanding. "Bed?"

"Yes, the thing we sleep on." *My God*, he thought, *what if I've given her the wrong drug? Maybe I jumped to the wrong conclusion about what Corcoran kept in the box*.

"I'll be up shortly," June said. "I'm just thinking about . . . everything."

"Look, I'm sorry about what happened earlier. I did it for *us*, you understand. It's a medical fact that overweight people develop an unreasoning fear of anything which threatens to . . ." Herley abruptly stopped speaking as he realised he had garnered his medical "fact" from some of Hamish Corcoran's wilder ramblings. He stared down at his wife, wondering if it could be only an effect of his disturbed mental state that she seemed more gross than ever, her head – in his foreshortened view – tiny in comparison to the settled alpine slopes of her body.

"Don't forget to lock up," he said, turning away to hide his repugnance.

When he got to bed a few minutes later the coolness of the sheets was relaxing and he realised with some surprise that he would have no trouble in falling asleep. He turned off his bedside lamp, plunging the room into almost total darkness, and allowed his thoughts to drift. The day had undoubtedly been the worst of his life, but if he kept his head there was absolutely nothing the police could pin on him. And as regards the trouble over the injections, June's attitude was bound to change by morning when she found there were no ill effects. Everything was going to be all right, after all . . .

Herley awoke very briefly a short time later when his wife came to bed. He listened to the sound of her undressing in the darkness, the familiar sighs and grunts punctuated by the crackle of static. When she lay down beside him he placed a companionable hand on her shoulder, taking the risk of the gesture being interpreted sexually, and within seconds was sinking down through layers of sleep, grateful for the surcease of thought.

The dream was immediately recognisable as such because in it his mother was still alive. Herley was two years old and his father was away on a business trip, so Herley was allowed to share his mother's bed. She was reading until the small hours of the morning and , as always when her husband was away, was eating from a dish of home-made fudge, occasionally handing a fragment to the infant Herley. She was a big woman, and as he lay close her back seemed as high as a wall – a warm, comforting, living wall which would protect him forever against all the uncertainties and threats of the outside world. Herley smiled and burrowed in closer, but something had begun to go wrong. The wall was shifting, bearing down on him. His mother was rolling over, engulfing him with her flesh, and it was impossible for him to cry out because the yielding substance of her was blocking his nose and mouth, and she was going to suffocate him without even realising what was happening . . .

Mother!

Herley awoke to darkness and the terrifying discovery that he really was suffocating.

Something warm, heavy and slimy was pressing down over his face, and he could feel the moist weight of it on his chest. He clawed the object away from his mouth, but was only partially successful in dislodging it because it seemed to have an affinity for his skin, clinging with the tenacity of warm pitch. His fingers penetrated its surface and slid away again on a slurry of warm fluids.

Whimpering with panic, Herley heaved himself up off the pillow and groped for the switch of the bedside light. He turned it on. From the corner of one eye he glimpsed what had once been his wife lying beside him, her naked body bloody and strangely deflated, the skin burst into crimson tatters. The horror of the sight remained peripheral, however, because his own body was submerged in a pale, glistening mass of tissue, the surface of which was a network of fine blood vessels.

He screamed as he tried to tear the loathsome substance away. It ripped into quivering blubbery strips, but refused to be separated from him, clinging, sucking, tonguing him in dreadful intimacy.

Herley stopped screaming, entering a new realm of terror, as he discovered that the slug-like mass was somehow penetrating his skin, invading the sanctum of his body.

He got to his feet, dragging the glutinous burden with him, and in a lurching, caroming run reached the adjoining bathroom. Almost of their own accord, his fingers located and opened the bone-handled razor, and he began to cut.

Heedless of the fact that he was also inflicting dreadful wounds on himself, he went on cutting and cutting and cutting . . .

Detective-Sergeant Bill Myers came out of the bathroom, paused on the landing to light a cigarette, and rejoined his senior officer in the front bedroom. "I've been in this business a hell of a long time," he said, "but those two are enough to make me spew. I've never seen anything like it."

"I have," Inspector Barraclough replied sombrely, nodding at the lifeless figure on the bed. "This is the way we found Hamish Corcoran's wife a couple of years ago, but we managed to keep the details out of the papers – you know how it is with false confessions and copycat murders these days. It looks as though we'll be able to close the file on that case, thank God."

"You think this man Herley was a psycho?"

Barraclough nodded. "He's obviously been lying low for a couple of years, but we've established that he went to Corcoran's house yesterday. Killing Corcoran must have triggered him off somehow – so he came home and did this."

"It's his wife I feel sorry for." Myers moved closer to the bed and forced himself to examine what lay there, his eyes mirroring unprofessional sympathy. "Skinny little thing, wasn't she?"

HUE AND CRY

Turbon stared fixedly at the mouth of the cave where the two-legged food creature was trapped. He had an uneasy feeling that something was beginning to go wrong with his plan, but was unable to decide what it could be.

His wife stirred impatiently, ripples of green morning sunlight running like water along her powerful body. "I still think we should send in a bunch of females," she said. "If the food creature does kill a couple of them it will be so much the better. You and I can have the food creature and the others can have the dead females."

Turbon suppressed a sarcastic reply. He had spent years building up his public image of the imperturbable Philosopher King, but there were times when Cadesk annoyed him so much he almost threw it all to the winds. For perhaps the thousandth time he wished fervently he had been born a female, in which case he would have destroyed Cadesk with one blow and – the ultimate insult – refused to eat her afterwards.

"Be calm, dearest. You mustn't forget that I have been listening to these creatures' radio transmissions for years while – I might point out – others were immersed in brutish pleasures. I *know* them. There will be about twenty others in the space ship . . ."

"The what?"

"The space ship."

"You mean the shell?"

"Yes, dearest, I mean the shell; but we must learn to think of it as something more than a food container – it is a machine which can fly from star to star, not just a large exoskeleton. As long as the trapped food creature is alive the others will not leave here. I expect them to emerge from the space ship at any moment and try to retrieve their companion – then, thanks to my wisdom, we will have twenty to share among us. I shall not be greedy, of course, perhaps two or three . . .

"Stop rambling," Cadesk interrupted coarsely. "I can't listen to you and that stupid shouting at the same time."

Turbon glanced up to where six males were crouched before the cave-mouth, emitting, in obedience to his orders, blasts of radio waves from their speech centres each time the food creature within tried to communicate with the space ship from which it had strayed. He wondered if he should try to explain something of what he had learned about the strangers who walked on only two legs.

Years previously, when he had first heard their voices filtering down from the sky, Turbon had believed he was listening to beings like himself who by virtue of strong metallic traces in their nervous systems were able to communicate by radio emission. It had been a long time before he realised his imagined giants who could shout from star to star were, in reality, only creatures who spoke with sound waves but employed radio to extend their range. The next big step forward had been the discovery that the creatures also transmitted pictures. After a year of intense mental effort and discipline – during which Cadesk had continually threatened to leave him because of the apparent loss of his sexual powers – he had learned to unscramble the signals and actually *see* the pictures from the sky. Once this breakthrough had been made Turbon got to know a lot about the unfamiliar creatures and had learned their language.

"If the shouting goes on much longer," Cadesk said petulantly, "I won't be able to eat."

Turbon ignored this comment, partly because it was such a blatant lie but mainly because he had realised what was going wrong. The creature had previously been making sporadic attempts to use its radio transmitter, but for the last few seconds the attempts had been coming very close together. The massed shouts from the six males, faithfully superimposing themselves on the signals from the cave, were forming a pattern of long and short bursts of radio noise.

He tugged Cadesk's tail in panic. "Get up near the cave at once and tell the males to shout continuously. No more of this starting and stopping. The food creature is using them to send its message." Cadesk gave him an exasperated glance, but she slid obediently away through the yellow undergrowth. At an early stage Turbon had learned the code which the sky creatures used for continuous wave transmissions and, with a sinking sensation, he applied it to the emergent pattern.

". . . *able to study these beasts for some time without their knowledge. The main thing to remember when you come for me is that only the females can kill. If you pick them off first the males will run for cover. They are easy to tell apart. In fact you cannot go wrong in identifying male and female because . . .*" The remainder of the message was drowned out as the six males, having been reached by Cadesk, swung over to producing an uninterrupted blast of noise. Turbon twitched with relief.

They held a meeting of the Elder Council right away. "That's it then," Cadesk said briskly when told the situation. "It would be stupid to try an attack now that the food creatures have our secret. I vote we rush the cave now and at least get *something*. I must say, also, that the creature wasn't long in deciding who matters and who doesn't around here." She flexed her great killer's muscles and lay down. The other five members of the Council, being male, registered as much protest as they dared but the general feeling of the meeting was that Cadesk had scored a definite point.

Turbon stepped into the breach quickly, aware that this was an important chance to demonstrate the superiority of mind over muscle. "It is true," he announced, "the food creatures are aware that our females invariably carry out the . . . less pleasant tasks associated with the perpetuation of our species, but . . ."

"Don't be too modest," Cadesk interrupted. "One of these days you'll learn how to talk 'em to death."

". . . but, important as this piece of information undoubtedly is, it's of little value to anyone encountering us for the first time. The differences in physiognomy, musculature, pigmentation, etc, which enable us to distinguish male from female so readily are meaningless without prior knowledge. In short, the food creatures can't tell one of our males from one of our females – so, in effect, nothing has changed."

Cadesk looked impressed. "He's right, you know. Perhaps we ought to keep to the original plan, but I hope something happens soon. I can almost smell them from here." She smacked her lips and drooled slightly in a way which Turbon, in spite of himself, found captivating.

In the afternoon of the following day something did happen. A door on the spaceship swung open and fourteen of the two-legged food creatures, carrying weapons, set out across the mile of jungle which lay between their ship and the cave.

The plan was immediately put into action. It was not a highly developed scheme because the Trelgans, as the dominant life form on a world of primitive jungle, were in the habit of simply running headlong at anything which moved and then eating it. But for Turbon's advice about weapons they would have done the same thing with the new arrivals from the sky. Instead they had devised what they felt was a subtle little manoeuvre – the idea being to hide behind trees until the strangers were in their midst and *then* run headlong and eat them.

When the big moment arrived the food creatures made it easy by following a dead straight line to the cave, moving slowly through the ochre vegetation, weapons at the ready, red uniforms catching the sun. Turbon and Cadesk had mustered all their forces for the attack – two dozen females and four times as many males. They even had time to find a good vantage point half way up a huge tree overlooking the scene of the ambush, which was a flat piece of ground quite close to the cave.

"You're certain nothing can go wrong?" The wait was straining Cadesk's naturally minute store of patience.

"Of course, dearest," Turbon replied peacefully. "The food creature told the others they would have no trouble identifying our females, but he didn't get the chance to say how. Perhaps, being mammals, they are assuming we are too, and will be looking for creatures with great lactic glands thumping about all over the place." He laughed at the idea and then fell silent as the

leaders of the little column of food creatures came into view at
the far edge of the clearing.

It seemed to take an eternity for the slow-moving file to reach
the centre but they finally made it and Turbon gave the signal to
attack.

Moving with beautiful precision the Trelgans emerged from
hiding and converged on the food creatures at top speed, their
hurtling bodies smashing smaller bushes and trees out of the way.
The strangers' weapons began to flash but Turbon noted with
satisfaction that the females were well spaced among the males,
and Cadesk almost fell from her perch in anticipatory excitement.

"Don't they smell good," she slobbered. "Tear 'em apart!"

Turbon smiled indulgently, then realised that he could now
only see about half the females who had started the charge. The
file of food creatures had contracted into an efficient little knot
and the sharp reports of their weapons were a continuous crash
of thunder. And the astonishing, ghastly truth was that they were
concentrating their fire on the widely-spaced females! Even as he
realised what was happening, the number of females withered
under the accurate shooting until there were only five . . .
four . . . three . . . two . . .

A solitary female escaped with the fleeing males as the charge
suddenly reversed its direction and raced outwards like the ripple
from a pebble dropped in water. Only ten hellish seconds had
elapsed since the beginning of the attack but in that time Turbon
had lost more than half of his subjects, including all but one
female. He was almost unable to believe it had happened. How
could it have happened?

"This is your fault," Cadesk snarled. "This wouldn't have
happened but for your big ideas. That settles it – from now on I
give the orders around here."

"But I don't understand it," Turbon protested numbly as the
file of food creatures re-formed and passed out of sight in the
direction of the cave. "The one we trapped gave absolutely no
information as to how the others could tell female Trelgans from
males. There was just no way they could have known!"

Cadesk slapped him across the face with her powerful tail. "Shut up and let's go," she snapped. "I'm hungry." They climbed down from the tree and together moved into the clearing where the survivors of the ill-fated charge were already returning to dine off their unlucky comrades. In spite of the great shock they had received Turbon and Cadesk still made a handsome couple by Trelgan standards, and the afternoon sun glinted on their sleek, heavy bodies.

On his blue body.

And her pink body.

THE K-Y WARRIORS

"Grandma Gina's fridge runs without being plugged into the electricity," Tommy Beveridge said, casually throwing the remark into a discussion about machines in general and the workings of the internal combustion engine in particular.

Willett Morris smiled indulgently at his nephew. "Some fridges run on gas."

"Yes, but she hasn't got gas." Tommy spoke with the assurance of a precocious eleven-year-old. "Grandma Gina is all-electric."

"Then her fridge *must* be plugged into the mains." Willett switched from car engines to the principles of refrigeration, determined to educate the boy into seeing how nonsensical his statement had been. But Tommy soon exhibited signs of boredom, darted out of the garage/workshop and began pursuing the butterflies that twinkled over the lawn. Willett was disappointed, thinking it a shame that nobody else in the family appreciated the beauty inherent in even the simplest machines.

He shook his head, returned to the workbench where – just for the sheer pleasure of it – he was rewinding a washing-machine motor, and the snippet of conversation quickly faded from his mind. It had seemed pointless and inconsequential in the extreme, and when he recalled it many months later it was unrecognisable as a prelude to sudden death.

There had been times, right at the beginning of Muriel's driving instruction, when Willett had believed himself to be enduring the worst extremes of misery and fear.

To take but one example, there had been the business of her control – or lack of control – of the clutch pedal. That period had lasted for a couple of months, and during it Muriel had, when trying to move off from standstill under the slightest hint of strain, simply taken her foot off the pedal and allowed it to spring up. Each time the car had bucked to a self-damaging halt and Willett, visualising shock waves racing through the transmission, had waited with sick apprehension for the metallic *thunk* and sudden roar of a freed engine which would have signalled a broken half-shaft. It had seemed miraculous to him that no component had ever actually failed, although he had no doubt that the car's mechanical life had been drastically shortened.

At least twenty times he had taken a deep breath and, while stoically staring straight ahead, had said, "You must bring the clutch pedal up slowly."

"There was a lorry coming," Muriel would say. "I had to get away quickly."

And at least twenty times Willett had replied, "Forgive me for being so dense about these things – but how does stalling the engine aid a quick getaway?"

The sarcasm had never had any noticeable effect.

Then there had been the occasions when, with a dangerous obstacle looming directly in front, he had snapped out the order to brake and had experienced an exquisite and soul-withering dread as the car had continued on its way, direction and speed unaltered, with Muriel apparently in a trance. The frenzied uncontrollable stamping of his right foot on a non-existent brake pedal at his side of the car had always startled her into last-instant action, followed by tears and recriminations about his lack of consideration for her nerves.

In retrospect those incidents, so harrowing at the time, were seen to be trivial and almost amusing – for now Muriel had progressed to driving in traffic. And, what was much worse, she had acquired a totally unwarranted confidence.

Please hurry up, Willett thought as he leaned against the car and surveyed the deepening colours of the sky. It was late on an April afternoon and he wanted the day's lesson to be completed before darkness fell, otherwise the risks to the vehicle and its occupants' health would be greatly increased. He glanced towards the house and detected a blurry movement behind the pebbled glass of the hall window which told him that Muriel was on the phone to her mother or one of her sisters. A good two hours had passed since the five women had met over tea and scones, and therefore it was necessary for them to be brought up to date on each other's activities before Muriel could leave the house.

Trying to control his impatience, Willett used the toe of his shoe to decapitate a small weed which had had the impertinence to thrust up through the gravel of his drive. What was it that Muriel had accomplished in the course of the afternoon which was so important that tidings of it had to be electronically circulated with the expensive help of British Telecom? All he had noticed her doing was giving the shower curtain its weekly wash. The curtain was a sheet of pink plastic whose sole function in life was to withstand repeated dousings with hot soapy water. At regular intervals Muriel decided it needed revivifying, a goal she sought to achieve by putting it in the Hotpoint and dousing it with hot soapy water.

Willett had long since given up criticising the procedure on the advice of Hank Beveridge, who had been married to Yvonne, the youngest of Muriel's three sisters. "You'll never win that kind of argument," Hank had counselled, "and your health will only suffer if you try. Hypertension, old son! That's the way women get you, you know. They kill you by making you kill yourself."

Willett still missed Hank for his black humour and cynical wryness, even though in the weeks before his death he had shown distinct signs of progressing beyond the socially acceptable degree of neuroticism. At lunchtime on most Sundays the two had met at the Rifleman's Arms – a pub which was equidistant between their homes and mercifully free of juke boxes and games machines – and had spent pleasurable hours in conversation. Declining standards in just about everything had been a favourite topic, and the essential strangeness of the female mind had been another.

"It's hard to find a fresh egg in my house," Hank had once said. "And do you know why? Yvonne refuses to keep them in the fridge. She thinks she read somewhere that eggs keep better at room temperature. But do you know what she *does* keep in the fridge? Pickles and preserves! The two kinds of food whose names are synonymous with imperishability! Our fridge is so full of pickles and preserves you can hardly get anything else in there, Willett, but I pass no comment. She's not giving *me* hypertension."

The last had been a reference to Clive and Edward, the deceased spouses of Yvonne's older sisters. Both men had died before their time of blockaded hearts, and afterwards Hank had never tired of elaborating on a fantasy based on the notion that the Sturmey sisters were a breed who consciously killed their husbands . . .

The sound of the front door being closed interrupted Willett's reverie. He raised his head and watched Muriel carefully making her way towards him on red sandals whose slim heels went deep into the gravel at every step. At the age of fifty his wife looked almost exactly as she had done in her twenties and could wear her daughters' clothes without exciting comment. Willett was not particularly aware of his own mortality, but there were times when he was shocked to realise that Muriel – with her temperate habits and long-lived forebears – might be only halfway through her span. Another life awaited her if he were to die soon.

She was of medium height and medium build and had what he thought of as a medium face, one which had nothing particularly wrong with it and which could be made quite beautiful when she took the trouble, which was most of the time. Today she was wearing a white blouse and white slacks, and had tied her black hair in place with a red-and-white scarf. He recognised the ensemble as one of her motoring outfits – she always changed her clothes specially for driving lessons.

"The afternoon's going," he said. "Who were you phoning?"

"Yvonne." Muriel got into the driving seat and began taking off her sandals.

Willett opened the passenger door and sat beside her. "But you were with Yvonne most of the day. What could you possibly have to talk about on the phone?"

"It was only a local call – it won't bankrupt you."

"I'm not bothered about the cost of the call. I'm genuinely

interested in finding out what you had to add to the day's deliberations. What were you talking *about*?"

"Women's things. You're being childish, Willett." Muriel rummaged below her seat, selected flat-heeled shoes from the three pairs she kept in a cluttter around the seat-positioning mechanism and worked her feet into them. Willett watched the performance with bafflement and, in spite of his best intentions, a growing annoyance. Would any man, anywhere, have thought of treating the car as a kind of travelling wardrobe?

"That's better." Muriel fastened her safety belt and switched on the ignition with the key Willett had left in the lock, illuminating the square plastic buttons on the dash. He waited for her to begin the ritual struggle with the handbrake, then became aware that she was staring at the instrument display as though never having seen it before.

"Willett," she said in tones of wonderment, "why is the little watering-can lit up?"

He closed his eyes in exaggerated disbelief. "What did you just say?"

"Are you going deaf? Why is the little watering-can lit up?"

"Are you by any chance," he ground out, "referring to the oil pressure warning light?"

"I don't care what you call it," she snapped. "Why is it lit up?"

Willett kept his eyes shut. "Muriel, are you telling me – after all the hours I've spent explaining the workings of the car to you – that you think the oilcan symbol is meant to be a watering-can?"

Muriel giggled. "How was I to know? It looks just like the little green one I use for the house plants."

"Oh, Jesus," Willett said, a painful acidity welling in his stomach.

"There's no need to blaspheme," Muriel said angrily. "And I don't care about your rotten old warning lights if you don't." She switched on the engine, released the hand-brake with her customary struggle and silent mouthings, put the car into gear and made a take-off so violent that it would have resulted in a stall had not the back wheels spun on the loose surface of the drive. Willett winced as the gravel spattered through his dwarf dahlias like grapeshot. On reaching the avenue Muriel turned left and drove towards the Bath Road, and now, suddenly, she was in an airy good humour.

"For goodness' sake try to relax, Willett," she said. "I don't want you having a heart attack on me."

Don't you? Willett thought, then realised he was in danger of becoming as paranoid as Hank had been at the end. For a moment his thoughts strayed towards his deceased friend . . .

Hank had refused point blank to have anything to do with his own wife's driving tuition – "That's sticking your head into the lioness's mouth, old son." – and had been fond of pointing out that it had been when he was teaching Beryl that Edward Cookson's silted-up cardiovascular system had finally clenched him out of existence.

"Beryl could have learned to drive ages ago, but she waited till Edward's health wasn't up to the strain. It was her ultimate weapon, you see – and that's why she refused to go to a driving school."

"Cobblers," Willett had said comfortably.

"You'll see I'm right! Just pray that Muriel never uses the same tactic against you, old son. If she ever asks you to give her driving lessons, don't hang around! Emigrate to Australia –that's what Edward should have done!"

Willett remembered Edward Cookson as an unnecessarily gloomy man, but he had redeemed himself to some extent by producing one beautifully mordant line concerning his experience with Beryl at the wheel. *Every time she stalled the engine she gave me an accusing look and switched on the windscreen wipers*. Willett and Hank had often smirked into their lunchtime pints as they savoured the amount of sheer bitterness, frustration and male misery distilled into that single sentence.

"He's letting her get to him," Hank had once predicted – accurately, as it turned out – while staring into the malty oracle of his tankard. "He's going to go the same way as old Clive. Mark my words!"

"But where's the sense in it?" Willett had protested humorously. "Why *should* middle-aged women want to do away with their husbands?"

"We become redundant, old son. You see, after a man has fathered the children a woman wants and has burned himself out in providing financial stability for the family he isn't needed any more. He's actually *in the way*. It's insurance policy time."

"So he gets murdered!"

"Murdered isn't too strong a word for it, though in most cases it's an instinctive thing. In the battle of the sexes women have observed that men are susceptible to stress, so that's the preferred weapon to be used against us, and they employ it effortlessly and naturally."

"Sometimes I think you're serious about all this," Willett had said. "Don't women ever suffer from stress?"

"They're built to withstand it – physically and mentally. Nature has given them the upper hand, old son. They can go on for ever." Hank had lowered his voice in case the inquisitive barmaid at the Rifleman's was trying to eavesdrop. "Look how easy it is for them in bed."

"*Bed*? I don't get you."

"When a man gets on a bit in years it's harder for him to do the job – and, what's more, it's obvious that he is having difficulties. Therefore it's a stressful situation for him, but not for the woman – no matter how old she is. All she needs is a crafty squirt of that K-Y jelly and for all intents and purposes she's as good as an eighteen-year-old.

"I tell you, Willett," Hank had concluded dolefully, "the cards are stacked against us."

Willett remembered having laughed aloud at that one, and he still thought of it as a prime example of Hank's quirky humour, perhaps because Hank had died a few days later . . .

Some four hundred yards ahead of the car the brake lights of a lorry beaconed a warning, their ruby brilliance enhanced by the shade of the avenue's overhanging trees. Willett glanced at his wife. Her face was calm, her eyes intent on the road. Reassured, Willett sent relaxation commands down through his body and waited for Muriel either to slow down or drift the car to the right. It continued in the left-hand lane, speed unchecked as it headed straight for the stationary lorry's tailgate, with Muriel staring directly ahead and looking as coolly professional as an airline captain.

How long dare I wait? The question yammered in Willett's head as diplomacy battled with the urge for self-preservation. The lorry's brake lights swam apart as their range decreased. Willett opened his mouth to shout a warning and in the same instant the lights went out, showing that the lorry driver had eased up on the brake pedal. The disappearance of the ruby suns somehow galvanised Muriel into belated action. She stamped on the brake and the car dipped to a halt with its nose almost below the lorry's mud-streaked tailgate.

"Did you see that?" Muriel turned to Willett with a scandalised expression.

"I certainly did," he said, over the clamour in his nervous system. His forehead and cheeks tingled coldly and he felt ill.

"No lights! No signals! I've a good mind to report that maniac to the police." Muriel backed the car a short distance and drove past the lorry, her head turned and tilted in an effort to spear the driver with a look of outrage. Willett considered telling her what had actually happened, but quickly relinquished the idea. Muriel would have been both disbelieving and furious, and another row would have a bad effect on her driving. He remained silent as she took the car to the end of the avenue and manouevred it into the Bath Road with an overt display of safety consciousness. Willett's heart rate was returning to normal, but his spirits sank when he saw that the out-of-town traffic was already building up. He had been hoping to get the excursion over and done with before the rush hour got under way.

"We were looking at brochures today," Muriel said, deciding to chat just when the greatest demands were about to be made on her concentration.

"How nice." Willett had no need to enquire about the content of the brochures. Gina Sturmey and the three daughters who had become widows were planning to go on an extended cruise next

winter, and the planning of it was already taking up much of their
time. Muriel sat in on all the sessions even though finances
precluded her going on the voyage, and the others had not
thought of making her their guest. Willett was not sure if it was
because possessing a living spouse set her apart from them to
some extent, or if they were simply being tight with their
inherited money. He had noticed that, no matter how unified by
mutual love the Sturmey women were, when it came to matters
of hard cash there was very little give and take. It was only
natural, he supposed, that anybody who had killed her husband
to get hold of his savings and insurance was not going to . . .

Stop it! he told himself. *You're straying into Hank's old fantasy
too often these days.*

"Yes," Muriel went on, "the four-berth cabins on the *Minora*
seem fabulous."

"*Four* berths? That's not so good, is it?"

"Why?"

"I thought the whole point of those ocean cruises was a spot of
the old shipboard romance. All four in one room is going to be a
bit awkward, unless they're thinking of group sex – and your
mum is a bit too old for that."

"Willett!" Muriel looked at him with disgust and, as always
happened when she took her eyes off the road, the car
immediately veered from its proper line.

"Watch that cyclist," Willett said urgently.

"You watch what you say about my mother. You've got a filthy
tongue, Willett Morris."

"It was only a joke," he said, vowing never again to distract his
wife while she was at the wheel. Muriel had once possessed a
strong sex drive, and he knew she had had several affairs after
their marriage cooled, but – like her mother and sisters – she was
ultra-prudish in her speech. He still remembered the occasion
when he had been describing a machine and had aroused her
curiosity with a reference to a female component. When he had
explained it was so called because a male component slid into it
she had accused him of being sex-crazed and had flatly refused to
believe that the terms were standard throughout the engineering

world. After he had proved the point with the aid of a parts catalogue her opinion of men in general had sunk to a new low.

In the remaining fifty minutes of the driving lesson Muriel punished Willett to the full for the tasteless remark concerning her mother and sisters. Her tactics included making near-homicidal raids on pedestrian crossings; performing dangerous right turns in the face of looming heavy goods vehicles; refusing to dip the head-lights after dark, thus instigating beam duels with a half-dozen other drivers; repeatedly switching on the starter motor when waiting at traffic lights, even though the engine was running, thereby whipping up the whole motive system into a humming frenzy; and – as a final masterstroke – loftily assuring him that he could cure a squeaking windscreen wiper by spraying it with UB40.

By the time the car had crunched backwards into the drive at home Willett had an invisible steel band around his chest, a giant Jubilee clip whose screw tightened with every word Muriel spoke. There was a brief respite for him after the car had stopped, because – in accordance with her own imponderable rules – Muriel remained in the vehicle to check her appearance in the mirror and to change her shoes for the ten-yard walk to the house. The delay gave him time to get to the whisky decanter in the sitting-room and gulp a half-tumbler of Bell's. He braced himself for the inevitable accusations of alcoholism, and was scarcely able to believe his luck when he heard the telephone dial whirring in the hall. Muriel was reporting in to her mother or one of the sisters, and – mercifully – he had time for another drink. He poured a second bumper, equivalent to about four pub measures, and was getting the last of it down him as Muriel came into the room.

"You're an alcoholic," she said briskly, but without concern. "I want you to pop over to Mum's house and borrow a bag of icing sugar. Not ordinary sugar – *icing* sugar. Can you remember that?"

"I think my brain can cope with that mammoth task," Willett said. "When do you want me to go?"

"Now, of course. You've nothing better to do, have you?"

Willett had been looking forward to reassembling the carburettor of his lawn mower before dinner, but consoled himself with the thought that going to Gina's would enable him to have another drink in the guilt-free atmosphere of the Rifleman's. "Nothing that can't wait," he said. "Have I time to walk? I feel like stretching the old legs."

"Just don't be late for dinner – we eat at seven." Muriel went upstairs to change out of her driving outfit, leaving Willett alone in the sitting-room. He glanced at the whisky, decided there would be little to be gained from another furtive drink, and set off on his errand. The air was mild and scented with greenery, and the trees in the avenue seemed to be artfully screening the streetlights, contriving new patterns of illumination for his benefit as he walked.

This is more like it, he thought, taking deep and pleasurable breaths. *Relax, relax, relax! That's the way to fight back against the K-Y warriors.*

He had two more glasses of Bell's in the orange-spangled cosiness of the Rifleman's and by the time he had completed the half-mile walk to Gina Sturmey's house was feeling reasonably fit and capable of dealing with his mother-in-law. Her house was a large detached affair, well over a century old, but although Gina was in her seventies she somehow managed to keep it clean and in good repair with very little outside assistance. A hall light shone through the leaded glass of the front door, suggesting that he was expected, but there was no response to his ringing of the bell. He rang twice more, then turned the door's ceramic handle and went inside. Faint illumination seeped from the upper reaches of the panelled stairwell and the rear of the house, where the kitchen was situated, was augmented by a whiter glow.

"Gina?" Willett called out. "Are you home?"

Feeling uncomfortably like a law-breaker, he went along the hall, through the unlit dining room and into the fluorescent brilliance of the empty kitchen. Reflective cupboards and counters reproached him for having entered their presence unbidden, warning him not to try searching for icing sugar without their owner's consent.

"*Gina!*" Willett shouted in aggrieved tones. He now felt like a prisoner in his mother-in-law's kitchen, because were he to venture into another part of the house he might startle her or – unthinkably – surprise her in a state of undress. Muttering disconsolately, he glanced around the square room and in that strange moment of isolation memory cells fired off a salvo in his brain, thus recreating a scene from the past.

Grandma Gina's fridge runs without being plugged into the electricity, little Tommy Beveridge had said one day last summer.

The notion was as ridiculous as ever, but it prompted Willett to take special notice of the refrigerator. It was rather large and old-fashioned, with rounded edges which made it look like something from a 1940s Hollywood movie. It hummed faintly, introspectively. Willett moved past it, bringing a wall socket into view, and saw at once that the refrigerator was not plugged in. The electrical flex from it trailed down to a narrow strip of flooring between the fridge and adjacent cupboard, terminating in a three-pin plug. Bemused, Willett hunkered down, picked up the plug and found its top to be loose. He selected an appropriate screwdriver from the four in the breast pocket of his jacket and opened the plug. The fuse was missing.

Willett stood up and looked behind the refrigerator, expecting to see alternate wiring leading to some other power source, but there was nothing of that nature visible. He opened the refrigerator's curvaceous door and the internal light came on, wanly illuminating glass shelves of jars, bottles and plastic boxes. Cold air flowed downwards over his ankles.

"This doesn't make sense," Willett muttered. He knelt on the floor and – using his pen-light – looked underneath the refrigerator, hoping to find evidence that some untutored maverick of an electrician had brought a power cable up through the floor, but again there was nothing to fulfil his expectations.

"There's something bloody haywire here," he said in a louder voice as he stood up and returned the flashlight and screwdriver to his pocket. He left the kitchen, returned to the hall and was about to shout up the stairs when he heard a movement on the landing. A moment later Gina Sturmey came into view wearing a tangerine jump-suit which had been designed for a younger generation, but which looked right on her trim 75-year-old figure. In the soft light she appeared no older than any of her daughters, and for an instant Willett was unaccountably afraid of her.

"Hello, Willett," she said, descending the staircase towards him. "I heard you at the door, but I was in the middle of varnishing my nails." She held up her hands and displayed nails the exact colour of her suit. "How are you these days?"

"I'm . . ."

"I'll fetch you the sugar," Gina cut in. "Muriel says she feels *so* silly over having forgotten to buy icing sugar, especially as we were looking at it in Sainsbury's only last week, but it was on Friday afternoon and the place was so crowded we could hardly move. I'm always telling her it's much better to shop early in the morning, but she says you can go *too* early and then the shelves haven't been properly restocked from the day before and you can . . ."

"There's something not right about your fridge," Willett said loudly. "Has some clever dick been working on it?"

Unexpectedly, Gina gave the classic Sturmey giggle. "Here I am talking about Muriel's bad memory – and mine is even worse! I meant to tell her to tell you to bring a fuse over with you, and it flew right out of my head. Be a darling, Willett, and take the fuse off the Hoover for me. I can do without the cleaner till tomorrow, but . . ."

"You don't understand," Willett interrupted. "Your fridge is running without being plugged into the mains."

"But that's impossible."

"You don't have to tell *me* it's impossible," Willett said. "But it's happening just the same – come and see for yourself."

Gina's expression was a blend of caution and concern. "Is this a joke?"

"Come into the kitchen!" Willett turned and strode towards the rear of the house, with Gina following. No sooner had he entered the kitchen's cloud-white brilliance than he realised the refrigerator had fallen silent, and a premonition told him it was no longer working. He pulled open the door and the convenience light did not come on, making the interior seem dim and cavernous.

"It was working a minute ago," Willett said, more baffled than ever. "I swear to you – it *was*!"

"You reek of whisky, Willett. How much have you had today?"

"Whisky has nothing to do with it. Put your hand inside the fridge – it's still *cold* in there."

"Of course it is," Gina said gently, as though instructing a child. "The insulation will keep it cold for hours after the power is lost."

"Spare me the elementary physics, you . . ." Willett stifled an insult, realising the incident was getting out of hand. The trouble was that he *knew* the refrigerator had been working without being connected to the mains, and the fact that Gina was so firm in her denials was an invert proof that she knew too. Why would she not admit it? What was it to her if a piece of domestic equipment had behaved freakishly? She knew next to nothing about machinery, and would probably have believed a technological fairy tale about the fridge's cooling-grid picking up energy from the nearest radio station – so why was she giving him no argument?

Willett gazed helplessly at Gina's neat, hard face, then inspiration came to him. His nephew had observed the phenomenon a good nine months earlier – a fact which demolished Gina's claim that the refrigerator had been without a conventional power-source for only a matter of minutes. How would she wriggle out of that one? He was opening his mouth to challenge Gina when the telephone warbled. It was only a pace away from him, mounted on the tiled wall, and the unexpected loudness of it made him jump.

Gina took the handset and spoke her number into it. She listened for a short time, nodding and making little sounds of agreement, then said, "Don't worry about the car, Muriel – the important thing is that *you're* all right. Cars can easily be mended."

On hearing his wife's name and references to car damage, Willett moved closer to the phone, his heart lapsing into a bumping and unsteady rhythm.

"Yes, he's right beside me," Gina said into the instrument. Her eyes were watchful as she handed it over to Willett.

"What have you done, Muriel?" he said harshly. "What have you done to my car?"

"That's all you think about! Your rotten old car!" His wife had gone on the offensive immediately, which meant she had done something costly. "It doesn't matter about me, does it? I could be seriously injured and you wouldn't even . . ."

"The car, Muriel! What happened?"

There was a brief silence, then Muriel said, "I decided to put it into the garage to save you doing it when you got back, and . . . and it wouldn't stop for me. When I pressed the brake the car went faster."

"When you pressed the brake the car went faster." Willett repeated the sentence in dull, noncommittal tones, hoping that merely hearing her own words would impress on Muriel just how nonsensical they were.

"That's what I said." Muriel sounded unrepentant.

Willett gave a deep sigh. "Muriel, if the car went faster you must have pressed the accelerator."

"Willett, I'm not stupid – I know the difference between the accelerator and the brake," Muriel said indignantly. "Anyway, your lathe got knocked over, and the back window of the car fell out."

"My lathe!" Suddenly the giant Jubilee clip was again in place around Willett's chest, squeezing inwards. "I'm coming home." He hung up the phone, brushed past Gina without speaking and headed for the front door.

"Haven't you forgotten something?" Gina called in his wake. "What about the icing sugar?"

"Stuff the icing sugar!" Willett snarled. Out in the avenue he set off in the direction of his house at a very fast walking pace, but within a few yards made the chastening discovery that the pressure in his chest had turned into actual pain. *That's the way they get you*, he could almost hear Hank Beveridge saying. *They kill you by making you kill yourself*.

He immediately slowed to an amble and began the measured breathing he had been told was an aid to relaxation. The pain in his chest subsided reluctantly, producing a flicker of discomfort every now and then as he made his way home through shallow drifts of fallen cherry blossoms. The candle-coloured lights of the Rifleman's beckoned in the distance, but he was not tempted. It had been a mistake, he now realised, to drink so much whisky in such a short time. The spirituous liquor was firing up his whole system just when it was imperative for him to be calm and cool. It had also given Gina the advantage of him, but then it had always been hard to best her in an argument. Look at the time . . .

Willett's pace slowed even further and a cool breeze seemed to touch his brow as his memory stirred again, projecting an image of the past on to the screen of the present. On his doctor's advice he had quit smoking more than ten years earlier, but he kept a large, urn-shaped lighter of solid silver on a bookcase in the living room. It contained neither batteries nor fuel, and was preserved purely as an ornament.

One Sunday afternoon, the summer before last, Willett had been tending the potted begonias on the rear patio while his wife entertained her mother and three sisters to tea. He had glanced in through the window just in time to see Anne – second youngest of the sisters – go to the bookcase, pick up the lighter and ignite her cigarette with it. Puzzled, because he did not think Muriel would have had the lighter serviced, he had gone into the house and examined it – and had found it still without batteries or fuel. When asked what he was doing Willett had related what he had seen through the window. For a moment Anne had seemed flustered, but Gina Sturmey had chimed in at that point with a scornful laugh, saying that Anne had already been smoking when she had casually picked up the lighter. Anne had quickly agreed with her.

Willett had not dared contradict the women when the facts were so plainly against him, but the image of Anne drawing flame from the lighter had always remained sharp in his mind, an irritating anomaly, a thorn in the flesh of reason and logic. And now, suddenly, a pattern was emerging – because the incident with the refrigerator was exactly the same kind of phenomenon.

Gina Sturmey and her daughters were witches who could make defunct machines operate as though they were in perfect condition!

"I've gone crazy," Willett announced to the empty street. "I'm worse than old Hank ever was!"

Paradoxically, the realisation of just how far he had strayed beyond the bounds of rationality served to ease his mind. He was an engineer, and he *knew* that he lived in an ordered universe, and the conclusion he had reached about his in-laws was an example of what could come from abandoning strict causality. Witches, indeed! Giving a self-deprecating snort, Willett tried to summon up some reserves of steadiness and commonsense. All right, so his wife had damaged the car and there was something he did not understand about an old refrigerator – was that sufficient reason to go round the twist or have a heart attack?

Besides, his theory about the Sturmey witches failed the most basic test in that it did not accommodate all the facts. Even if he discarded the antique notion of witchcraft and enlisted the aid of modern jargon terms like "psi powers", he had not explained why Gina and her brood were so spectacularly inept when it came to machinery or anything technical. If they had a natural or supernatural ability to impress their will directly on machines, they ought to display an effortless mastery of all such objects. Or should they? Would that not be giving the game away?

Willett snorted again in the scented darkness as he entered the spirit of the mental game he had just discovered. No thinker liked to abandon a neat theory without a struggle, and here was an intellectual challenge – reconcile the Sturmeys' covert affinity with machines and their overt lack of such affinity.

There was a contradiction there, but did it really exist? Did it baulk in his mind because he was making the mistake of thinking as a man who had always been fascinated by engineering? His wife in particular seemed to have an antipathy towards all things mechanical, but what if that was according them too much importance in her scheme of things? She would not hate anything she saw as insignificant – she would simply regard it with disdain. All the Sturmeys could be the same. When it was necessary or convenient they might cause a broken machine to do their bidding, by one means or another, but for the sake of a quiet life they would not flaunt their power in the faces of their husbands and the world at large. The poor male spouses, exemplified by Willett, clinging to their cherished illusions of superiority, might not be able to stand it if all their hard-won understanding of torque and templates, degaussing and differentials amounted to nothing beside their wives' instinctive and casual mechanical wizardry.

That's not bad, Willett told himself, nodding in satisfaction. *Perhaps I should take up writing fantasy stories as a hobby. I wouldn't mind seeing my name on one of those paperbacks in Smith's (comparable to Tolkien at his best), but the theory is still incomplete.*

All right, let us suppose that the Sturmeys are modern witches, psi superwomen, and want to be discreet about it – why do they deem it necessary to go so far in the opposite direction and appear to be technological dunces? Take Muriel as an example. If she wants to learn to drive why doesn't she do so with remarkable competence, rather than put on a show of being so monumentally inept?

"I'm surprised you even bother to ask that question, old son," said the ghost of Hank Beveridge, conjured up and made almost tangible by the vividness of Willett's memory. "You've become redundant. Perhaps it's because Muriel would like to go with the others on that winter cruise, but – whatever the reason – she has decided you're for the high jump. It's the insurance policy time. I warned you about the driving lessons, old son. The ultimate weapon! She's killing you by making you kill yourself . . ."

"Cobblers," Willett muttered, disappointed by his failure to build a satisfactory armature of logic to support the witch theory at his first attempt. There was no time for a second try because the game was over – he was coming within sight of his own house and the glimmer of the garage lights was a reminder of what was waiting for him there.

In spite of all his sensible resolutions, he was unable to prevent an anxious quickening of his pace over the last hundred yards and was breathing heavily by the time he entered the driveway. Muriel was waiting under the porch light. She had changed her clothes and was now wearing a grey pullover, grey tweed skirt and low-heeled shoes.

That must be her I've-just-crashed-the-car outfit, Willett thought bitterly, wondering how his wife could concern herself with her appearance at a time of crisis. He nodded with grave courtesy as he passed her, calculating that a show of forbearance would increase her burden of guilt, and went into the garage. An involuntary moan escaped his lips as he saw that the lathe had not only been knocked over – it had been driven against the wall so hard that several breeze-blocks had been displaced outwards. The rear end of the car had been crunched into an expensive new free-form shape and the hatchback window, miraculously intact, was lying on the floor beside it. Willett's lower lip began to tremble while he was surveying the full extent of the catastrophe, but he brought it under control as Muriel entered the garage and came to his side.

"Thanks a lot," he said. "This is a nice little home-coming present."

"Don't be sarcastic with me, Willett Morris," she snapped. "It was all the fault of your stupid old car."

"Are you going to persist with this crap about the car going faster when you pressed the brake?"

"That's what happened. It must be something to do with a . . ." Muriel paused, rummaging through her small vocabulary of engineering terms. ". . . a linkage."

"Linkage! You haven't the foggiest bloody idea what you're talking about, woman." Willett was unable to prevent his voice ascending in both pitch and volume. "You pressed the wrong bloody pedal – and you haven't even the bloody decency to apologise."

"Apologise!" Muriel faced up to him and, far from being

apologetic, her eyes were bleak and baleful in a way that was outside his previous experience. "Why don't you get in and drive the car yourself? Why don't you prove me wrong?"

"That's easily done," Willett shouted, aware that the steel hoop was remorselessly crushing his chest. Ignoring the pain, he got into the driving seat, slammed the door and switched on the engine with the key Muriel had left in the lock. He revved up loudly to express his fury, put the car in gear and sent it surging out of the garage. Halfway along the drive he stamped on the brake, intending to give a spectacular demonstration of the car's stopping ability, but to his horror the vehicle leapt forward with frightening power.

Willett was unable to control the reflex which caused him to bear down on the brake pedal with all his strength. The engine roared and the car hurtled between the gate posts, gaining speed all the while, crossed the avenue in an instant and mounted the opposite footpath. Willett barely had time to see the stone wall which spanned the view ahead, before the appalling impact drove him against the steering wheel. Two sources of pain, one external and one from within, fused in his chest, going beyond what was humanly endurable as his body bounced and broke and finally came to rest in a grotesque kneeling position beneath the dashboard.

Willett found himself with his face almost jammed against the instrument panel, and the car – as though rewarding him for all the attention he had lavished on it – began to put on a light-show to entertain him during the final seconds of his life. One by one the lights came on, plastic tablets glowing with cheerful colours, and there among them was the oil pressure warning light with its picture of an oilcan. Seen from a distance of only a few inches, the symbol loomed large in his field of vision, exhibiting fine details he had never noticed before. Very oddly – for an oilcan – its spout ended in what looked like the perforated spray head of a watering can.

Muriel, don't do this to me, Willett pleaded inwardly, drowning in blood, as he saw the can begin to move. It tilted itself and sprinkled droplets of water over a stylised daisy. The daisy became invigorated, with Disney-style quiverings, and strained up towards the sun . . .

But by that time Willett was dead, and Muriel was hurrying to telephone her mother.

DISSOLUTE DIPLOMAT

Gringledoonk lay in a comfortable floor dish, experimenting with himself out of sheer boredom. From three points along his perimeter he projected slim pseudopods, intertwined them for a short distance in the centre, then split the end of each in two and looped them out to form six little hooks.

Listlessly he solidified the edifice and extruded an eye to examine it. It did not look like much.

There were several races in the Federation who covered their bodies with fabrics, and this thing he had made might have been useful to one of them, but not to anybody civilised. More bored than ever, he commenced the slow process of dissolving the hardened pseudopods.

A low whistle came from the entrance of the tubeway in the palace wall. The little circular door opened and Mugg, his Minister of Home Affairs, shot out on to the floor. He lay for a moment in the bullet shape that Gyoinks used for travelling the tubeway; then he re-formed and flowed into the floor dish beside Gringledoonk.

When he had stopped rippling, Mugg extruded an eye and, on seeing the peculiar shape his ruler had assumed, kept popping out more and bigger eyes to get a better view. Gringledoonk watched the process with disgust. No matter how often he was told about it, Mugg never seemed to realise how ill-mannered such displays of curiosity were.

"What," Mugg finally enquired, "have you done to yourself, Your Softness?"

"Never mind that," Gringledoonk said irritably. "Why did you come here? You know this is my rest period."

"It's important," Mugg replied. "A spaceship on normal drive has entered the system and is heading for this planet."

For an instant Gringledoonk lost the cool green colouring that befitted his position and allowed his natural mottled orange to show through. "*What*? What sort of a spaceship?"

"It appears to be a Terran ship, Your Fluidity."

"The Treaty does not allow Terran ships to land here," Gringledoonk said. "This is most unexpected. We'll have to check the libraries on how to receive the officers of a Terran ship."

He moved out of his dish, balancing the still rigid tripod with difficulty, and into the entrance port of the tubeway. The soft, warm radiance there helped him dissolve and reabsorb the cumbersome extension, and he vanished into the narrow aperture of the tubeway.

After years of inactivity, Gringledoonk, Lord and Representative of the Gyoinks, was back in business.

Hal Portman was holding a moderate 800C when his warp-drive generators gave a low sigh and vanished into some unknown dimension. The ancient Morris Starcruiser emerged into normal space with a sickening jiggle.

On checking his position, Portman found that there was a planet called Yoink so close, astronomically speaking, that he could have spat on it. He tapped out Yoink's coordinates on his destination selector and began drinking beer in preparation.

Two days and thirty-two cans of beer later, the Starcruiser bulleted down for a landing.

Wiping white froth from his bristly upper lip, Portman opened the lock and went down on to springy yellow turf. He found himself surrounded by a varicoloured crowd of beings of indeterminate shape who chittered at him excitedly. He could not decide whether their agitation was due to the sudden appearance of his ship or the fact that it seemed to have crushed a number of their plastic buildings on arrival.

He drew his sidearm and shouted, "Silence, friends. I am a citizen of – uh – Imperial Earth and I command your obedience. I want –"

One of the waist-high cones of jelly interrupted him by

sprouting an enormous mouth and bellowing something about violations of the Treaty. Portman gave the little alien a short burst from his Colt .45 which reduced it to a pile of crackling cinders.

"You're only saying that because you're jellos," he joked hastily, feeling that it might be better to pass the incident off. The directory had stated that the Gyoinks were non-aggressive, but there was no point in not acting in a friendly manner. He knew about the Treaty, but the cargo of contraband luminous furs that he had tucked away would have caused unwelcome comment if he had waited for an AA repair ship.

"Now listen, *friends*," he repeated, brandishing the weapon. "We'll get along as long as nobody argues or tries to get funny. My ship has broken down. Replace the warp generators and I'll be on my way."

"Imperial Earth will be grateful," he added as an afterthought. This diplomacy stuff was a cinch for a guy who knew how to handle people and things.

Several of the Gyoinks immediately extruded stumpy legs and waddled up the ramp into the ship. Others went off toward a larger domeshaped building, muttering something about going for tools.

Portman went into the ship and obtained a further supply of beer, booting aside any of the Gyoinks who got in his way, then lay down on the bright turf and contentedly watched the work progress. In spite of the fact that the Gyoinks were just animated trifles, he had to admit that they were pretty good space-drive mechanics.

Later in the afternoon as Portman sat on the ramp, smoking under the brilliantly pink sky, a Gyoink approached from the direction of the town on the horizon. This was a large, pale green Gyoink who looked unfamiliar to Portman.

"What do you want? You're disturbing a representative of Imperial Earth."

"I know, I know," the Gyoink replied humbly. "My name is Gringledoonk."

"Anything to the Boston Gringledoonks?" Portman queried genially.

"No," Gringledoonk said, wincing slightly. "I come to apologise for the conduct of my people earlier. When I heard that you were here, I came from the Capital to make sure you would receive the proper attention due to a representative of –"

"Yeah, yeah, I should think so," Portman cut in. "One of those jellos argued with me today. Argued! How do you like *that*?" He took the cigar from between his thick lips and pursed them in disapproval.

"Most regrettable," the Gyoink agreed. "I can assure you there will be no more such incidents. My people are ignorant of the formalities involved in the reception of the captain of a Terran ship. Fortunately, our libraries contain something about the traditions of the great Earth space fleets and, from now on, we will observe those traditions to the best of our limited ability."

"That's more like it," Portman said.

It had been necessary to dismantle the ship's power plant and, as the Yoink nights were chilly and the installation of the new generators would not be completed until the morning, Portman was moved into one of the little plastic huts about a mile from the ship. He found that the Gyoinks had rigged up a hammock, of all things, but it took him only a short while to find the knack of sleeping in it.

In the morning he was wakened by the sound of bells and the insistent prodding of a Gyoink who was proffering a glass of brown liquid on a small tray. The Gyoink's shiny surface had become bright blue. Portman demanded to know what was going on.

"Eight bells, sir," the Gyoink replied. "Your breakfast is ready." There was a note of eager sincerity in the Gyoink's voice.

Portman stretched luxuriously in the hammock, took the glass and found that the Gyoinks had contrived to produce a pretty fair rum. Grinning with satisfaction, he got up and lumbered out of the hut, stooping to get through the low door.

Outside, a flat open conveyance on four wheels, manned by two more blue Gyoinks, was waiting. It looked brand new and had lifebelts slung along the sides.

"The Chief Engineer reports that your ship is ready, sir," one of the Gyoinks said. "Step aboard and we will take you to it, sir. Aye, aye, sir."

Portman got into the car and sat down. As he was being driven the short distance to his ship, he found himself almost wishing that he was not leaving so soon. Once the jellos had come to understand that he was the boss, they had been all right, in spite of being such ugly brutes.

When they arrived at the battered old Starcruiser, Portman hardly recognised it. Its hull was shining with a rich brassy brilliance in the morning sunlight. Gringledoonk was waiting for him on a little platform at the foot of the ramp up to the airlock. Other bright blue Gyoinks stood in quivering rows nearby.

"Good morning, sir," Gringledoonk said, his voice charged with friendliness. "I hope that the launch we constructed for you was comfortable."

"The launch? Oh, yeah – very smooth. One of the jellos said the ship was ready. Is it?" Portman stepped out on to the platform.

"Everything is shipshape, sir," the Gyoink said. "We are doing our humble best to do everything in accordance with –"

"Yeah, I know. Skip all that stuff. As long as the new generators are in, I'll be satisfied."

"There's just one more thing, sir," Gringledoonk said. The ranks of Gyoinks moved aside, revealing a shallow depression in the platform, in the centre of which was a circular hole about six inches in diameter. From under the depression a plastic tube led up the ramp and into the ship.

"What, *what*?" Portman snarled.

"We only use this for long distances, but our library –"

"Skip it," Portman said.

He pushed Gringledoonk aside and headed for the bottom of the ramp across the dish-shaped hollow. Too late he noticed that there was a peculiar radiance hovering above the depression, coming from little translucent panels around its perimeter. He tried to retreat.

But his bones had softened too rapidly and indeed his feet were already flowing out of his shoes on to the floor, to be joined by what had been his legs and the remainder of his unwashed body. He stopped screaming as his head completed its gracious descent, and his staring eyes remained visible only for a moment, silently surveying the surface of the great blob which he had so unaccountably become. It liquefied still further and the mortal remains of Harold Portman ran out through the hole in the basin with a regrettably undignified noise. The plastic pipe became dark and murky as he passed up it into his ship.

"Just a matter of tradition," Gringledoonk explained proudly to the onlookers. "Our records are incomplete about Terran space fleet tradition, but they all agree on one thing – the Captain is always piped on board."

WELL-WISHER

Ibn Zuhain, Lord of the Long Valley, walked through the evening shade of his private garden. Beyond its filigreed triple walls the desert sand and rocks retained the oven-fierce heat of the day, but within Zuhain's sanctum the air was thick and fresh, seeded with moisture from a centrally placed fountain of elaborate design. The water, drawn from a deep-lying spring, was so cold that as Zuhain approached the cascade he could feel himself breasting concentric rings of coolness. This, he knew, was yet another form of Allah's bounty, and he was smiling his appreciation of it when he noticed a small blue flask sitting on the fountain's onyx rim.

He examined the bottle without touching it and saw it was a poor thing, imperfectly glazed and sealed with resin, most certainly not one of his own possessions. Its presence meant that an intruder had entered the private garden.

Zuhain sighed heavily, both irritated and saddened by the fact that he would now – on an evening which should have been entirely devoted to prayer and pleasure – have to order one or more executions. He had no relish for seeing trained servants beheaded, but they all knew the punishment for failing in any duty, and to withhold it would be to encourage sinful laxity.

Using the hem of his robe, Zuhain swept the offending bottle off his fountain and let it smash on the bright tesserae of the courtyard. He turned and strode away, intent on summoning the captain of his guard, but had taken only a few paces when – incredibly – a voice sounded behind him.

"Why such haste, my lord?" it said. "Are you so rich and powerful that there is nothing more in all of creation that you desire?"

Zuhain swung round, his hand on the ornate dagger at his

waist, and saw a tall man of Persian or Indian appearance regarding him with a smile. The stranger's calm, relaxed manner was both an insult and a threat – an assassin had to be very sure of himself to retain such composure – and Zuhain glanced about him, wondering if all his guards and servants could have been overpowered without his knowing.

"I am alone and wish you no harm," the stranger said, apparently divining Zuhain's thoughts.

"Tell me why you are here – before I have the pleasure of slaying you," Zuhain said.

"From me you can have the pleasure of three gifts – anything you desire – but nothing more." The stranger was standing close to the fountain and its spray shimmered colourfully all around him, making it difficult to see him clearly.

"You may be alone, but I am not," Zuhain assured him, "and from me you can have but one gift – that of death."

"Death? For me?" The stranger's smile grew broader. "The 'Lord of the Long Valley' must be a powerful ruler, indeed."

"Where have you come from?" Zuhain snapped, not liking the other's manner.

The stranger disturbed some blue shards with his sandal. "Must you ask?"

"I must."

"Then there can be no answer. Come, my lord, my time is short – state your first wish."

"My first . . ." Zuhain narrowed his eyes, trying to eliminate the luminous haze which blurred the intruder's outlines, and old memories began to stir. He held up his left hand, which had been injured eight years earlier and since that time, despite all the efforts of his physicians, had steadily withered into the semblance of a mummified claw.

"Restore this hand," he said, "and I will know who – or what – you are."

"It is done," the stranger replied carelessly.

Zuhain opened his hand, the fingers spreading like the petals of a long-dormant flower, and comprehension blossomed likewise in his mind. Allah was indeed favouring him above all other men, for here was his chance to be young again and – with the vigour of youth allied to the wisdom of age – to spread his kingdom to the limits of Islam and far beyond. Much though he wanted to shed the burden of his years, however, Zuhain's restless mind was drawn by another and, to him, more alluring prospect. History was one of the passions of which he was still capable, and he devoted himself to it, not for what it taught him about the past, but for what it enabled him to teach himself about the future. He saw the world as being in a state of continuous change, and it was one of his principal regrets that life was too short to allow more than a glimpse of the mighty spectacle of the Sons of the Prophet triumphantly carrying the true faith to the ends of the earth. But now, suddenly, it was within his power to soar like an eagle above the hidden landscapes of times to come.

"Tell me," Zuhain said to the stranger, "what is your name?"

The tall figure's eyes gleamed. "Is that your second wish?"

"Do not jest with me."

"Very well, my lord – you can call me Emad."

Zuhain pointed at him with a steady finger. "Emad, I command you to show me the world as it will be a thousand years from this day."

The stranger shook his head. "It would be well for you to understand that I cannot be commanded to do anything – not even by the Lord of the Long Valley. I am required only to grant you three wishes."

"Is it within your power to show me the world as it will be?"

"It is – but is that your second wish?"

"That is my . . . wish."

"Very well, my lord. *See!*"

Emad gestured at the floor of the courtyard between them, and suddenly the mosaic designs began to move, acquiring the fluidity and depth of a clear and sunlit sea. Zuhain found himself looking down on the familiar hills and valleys which surrounded his own capital, but vast and disturbing changes had been wrought. Of the thriving centre of commerce nothing remained but a scattering of shabby, ill-constructed huts, and the once-busy harbour had degenerated into a refuge for a handful of neglected fishing boats. Most vexatious was the fact that on the site of his own palace there remained nothing but a vague outline of the foundations, with streamers of white sand drifting across them like smoke.

Under Zuhain's mesmerised gaze the scene began to shift, and within the space of a few minutes he had visited all the far-flung territories of his fore-fathers and had ranged beyond them to the ocean of the east and the narrow sea of the west. In all of Arabia the picture was the same – one of poverty and degradation, of wasted farming lands, of sparse, dispirited communities in which the people scratched for a living amid the ruins of their former greatness.

"What devil's trick is this?" Zuhain's voice was cold. "What false visions are you showing me?"

"I have nothing to gain by deceiving you," Emad said emotionlessly, though his eyes had flashed again in what might have been anger. "This is your world as it will be a thousand years hence. This, Ibn Zuhain, Lord of the Long Valley, is the extent of your achievement."

"I warn you," Zuhain whispered fiercely, "your tawdry tricks will not avail you if . . ." He paused for a moment, his attention caught by a detail in one of the bright panoramas unfolding below. A caravan was climbing a mountain road, and to Zuhain's amazement he discerned that it was composed of large wheeled vehicles which moved – as though by magic – without the aid of any beast of burden. On the side of each vehicle was a white square upon which had been painted a red cross. The scene expanded until Zuhain could clearly see men inside the marvellous conveyances, and his nostrils flared as he realised they were infidels – sleek, well-fed, arrogant infidels, journeying without fear where they would once have been cut down and fed to dogs.

"What now?" Zuhain breathed. "What is the meaning of this?"

"It is quite simple, my lord." A hint of malice was now audible in Emad's voice. "The world is very large, and it has many lands where the sun does not burn so furiously, where there is water in abundance – and the future belongs to the peoples of those green lands."

"Do not lie to me," Zuhain commanded, gripping his dagger.

"See for yourself, Ibn Zuhain." Emad moved his right arm and the conjured scenes began to change with bewildering rapidity. Zuhain's senses were numbed by the succession of glowing images of proud, teeming cities, endless expanses of ripening crops, lush forests, bustling ports. And everywhere he looked great vehicles of commerce plied the roads, huge ships moved on the surface of the oceans without wind or sail, and he even saw machines which flew above the clouds like metal birds. The pageant was one of wealth, luxury and power.

"I hope my lord is satisfied," Emad said pointedly, showing signs of impatience. He gestured again with his arm and the floor of the courtyard returned to its former solidity. "It is time for your third wish."

"Not yet." Zuhain considered what he had seen, and his mind, skilled in the grasping of essentials, returned to the one factor which had been common to all the visions laid out before him. "Those ships I saw, the wagons, the machines which flew – what made them move? I saw no sails, no horses or camels, no tethered birds."

"All conveyances will propel themselves by means of engines."

"That is no explanation – what force is harnessed?"

"The force of the blue crystals, my lord."

"What crystals do you speak of? Sapphires? Amethysts?"

"You have no name for them because, although they are plentiful in other lands, almost none can be found throughout the length and breadth of Islam. Suffice it to say that the blue crystals have a power which in one respect is even greater than mine – they cannot be confined. Place one in the stoutest bottle or brass-bound cask and it will soon burst the top or sides. And as you have seen, men will learn to harness that power and make it serve them in many ways. In that age the lowliest peasants will be as rich as princes.

"And now," Emad concluded, "for your third and final wish. I assume that, like all the others, you desire the restoration of your youth and virility."

"Not so quickly – I saw no riches in my domain, nor in any part of Arabia."

"I have explained that the blue crystals are not found here, but do not alarm yourself, my lord." Emad's voice had taken on a caressing quality. "The other nations will be generous with gifts of food and medicine. Your children will not be allowed to starve."

Zuhain partially drew his dagger. "If you value your life, dog, do not speak in that manner."

"I tremble," Emad replied sarcastically, drawing himself up until he stood almost as high as the garden's central fountain. "Hurry, old man, state your wish. How young do you wish to be? Twenty? Fifteen?"

"As you say, I am an old man," Zuhain replied, checking his anger. "There is little time remaining to me, and it would be good to taste the sweet honey of youth once more – but what is a lifetime when measured against eternity? The seventy years you offer will draw to a close just as surely as those I have already spent."

"What if I offer you eternal life?"

"I have no desire to be forever denied entrance to Paradise."

"You are a fool, Ibn Zuhain," said Emad. "What, then, is your last wish?"

"I command you to rid this world of your accursed blue crystals and give me an equally powerful talisman in their place."

There was a pause before Emad replied, and when he did so his voice seemed hushed. "Even for you, even for the Lord of the Long Valley, such ambition is too . . ."

"*Do as I say!*" Zuhain thundered, drawing his dagger and throwing it at the towering silhouette. There was a flash, a ripple of shadow across the sky, and Emad was gone.

Zuhain looked all about him, anxious to behold the treasure for which he had eschewed eternal youth, and his shoulders sagged as he realised he had been betrayed. There was no treasure, no glittering talisman which would give his descendants the key to the wonderful future he had glimpsed. It occurred to him that he would have gained much had he treated Emad with politeness and consideration, but that had never been his way.

Dejected and angry, lost in his thoughts, Zuhain turned to leave the private garden, and at that moment there came a subtle alteration to the music of the high fountain. He looked at it and his eyes narrowed in fury as he appreciated the full extent of the jinn's trickery and malice.

The clear water of the fountain – solace of his fading years – had dried up, and in its place there gouted forth a black and evil-smelling oil which, already, had begun to disfigure everything in its vicinity.

EXECUTIONER'S MOON

"Wake up," Mike Targett shouted, his voice thick with excitement. "The computer thinks there's a village ahead of us!"

Dave Surgenor roused himself from a light doze, sat up straight in the left-hand seat of *Module Five* and looked out through the forward screen. The survey vehicle was skimming along at maximum speed, one metre above the surface of Korrill IV, and the view was the same as it had been for days. Beneath a sky which was crowded with vari-coloured moons, a flat snow-covered plain stretched from horizon to horizon, featureless and utterly devoid of life.

"Either you or the computer has a wire loose," Surgenor said. "And probably it's you."

"I'm *telling* you, Dave. Listen to this." Targett touched a button and the computer, which had been muted to allow Surgenor to sleep, began to speak more loudly.

"Receiving atypical data," it droned. "Receiving atypical data."

"Repeat the details," Targett said, with a triumphant glance at his partner.

"Five hundred kilometres ahead of you is a deep, narrow valley," the computer responded. "It runs in a generally north-south direction. Preliminary analysis of gases in the area indicates the presence of vegetation. Refined metals are also present which, together with traces of combustion products, indicates a small colony of intelligent beings possessing rudimentary technology."

"Hear these words," Surgenor said quickly, using the code phrase which gave him access to Aesop, the central computer aboard the mother ship, *Sarafand*. "What do we do next?"

While waiting for a reply he winked at his younger companion, consciously acting out the part of the veteran space traveller who had lost the capacity to be surprised at anything. But his heart had begun a steady, powerful pounding . . .

Korrill IV had presented special difficulties for the crew of the *Sarafand*, a Mark Six survey vessel of the Cartographical Service.

Standard operating procedure was that the mother ship would land at a planet's south pole and allow six survey modules to disembark. The mother ship, entirely under the control of its computer, then took off, did a half-circuit and landed at the north pole. Its survey modules did the same journey on the surface, equally spaced around the planet, all the while transmitting data to the ship for inclusion in the planetary resources map being constructed on the computer deck.

In normal circumstances the ship would complete its half-circuit of the planet in about an hour, in contrast to the survey crews who had to spend days toiling across the surface. Standard procedure had not been feasible in the case of Korrill IV, however, because the planet was surrounded by a shell of forty-three major moons and approximately four hundred minor natural satellites.

The *Sarafand* had spent a long time waiting for suitable 'windows' – gaps in the ever-changing screen of satellites – to enable it to land at the south pole and get away again. And now with the survey half-completed, it was parked in a safe orbit, awaiting its chance to put down at the north pole for its rendezvous with the survey modules.

In all of Surgenor's many years with the Cartographical Service that situation had cropped up only once before, and now another equally freakish event was occurring. The Service was only assigned to map worlds which were believed to be uninhabited, and it was a very rare event indeed for the survey crews to stumble across signs of intelligent life.

"How does anybody survive in a place like this?" Surgenor said, shivering as the icy wind bit through his protective clothing. He glanced wistfully back at the beetle-shaped outline of *Module Five*, which was already obscured by swirls of dry snow.

"It'll be a lot warmer when we get down into the valley," Targett replied. "Aesop says the temperature could be as high as fifteen degrees."

"Let's hope he's right." Surgenor advanced to the rim of the cliff which ran from north to south as far as the eye could see. He looked over the edge and, in spite of his foreknowledge, caught his breath as he saw the vivid greenery which lay far below. The valley was like something out of a fairy story, a magical oasis of lush vegetation and warmth in an arctic wasteland.

"They were lucky," Targett said. "If the people down there are the survivors from a crashed ship, as Aesop thinks, they were dead lucky to find this place before they froze solid."

Surgenor shook his head. "It didn't have to be pure chance. They could have detected the valley from space and maybe used their last remnants of control to bring their ship down in this area." Signalling for Targett to follow him, he walked along the cliff until he came to a place where the fall of the ground was less abrupt and carefully began his descent. They had been working their way down the hillside for only a few minutes when the icy conditions gave way to a region of bare rock, and then to grass and large clumps of shrubs. Soon the two men found it necessary to lower their parkas and remove their thermal jackets.

"At this rate we'll make it to the valley floor in twenty minutes or so," Surgenor said, glancing back at Targett and noticing that the younger man had unsheathed his ultralaser sidearm. "What's the artillery for? You feeling nervous?"

"I'm not taking any chances," Targett said. "I still think about that time on Horta VII when I found those killer robot torpedoes and nearly got my head shot off."*

"This is an entirely different situation." Surgenor shook his head in amusement. "I think that after being stranded on this ball of ice for a lot of years, these people will welcome us with open arms."

*Ship Of Strangers, Gollancz 1978

"I guess you're right," Targett said, lowering the weapon back into its holster. He had barely done so when there was a faint whizzing sound and a small dark object about the size of a wasp struck him on the neck. He gasped and clapped his hand over it and then, looking very surprised, sagged down on to the grass like a puppet whose strings had been released.

"What the . . . !" Surgenor grabbed frantically for his own ultralaser as he detected a movement in nearby shrubs, but in that instant something stung his arm. He just had time to see that it was a tiny dart as all the strength departed his limbs and he collapsed on the sloping ground.

A few seconds later a group of bearded men emerged from the cover of the bushy vegetation.

There were about ten of them, wearing only loincloths and carrying blowpipes and spears. Their bodies were streaked with green and yellow pigments which had enabled them to blend perfectly with their surroundings. They advanced silently and formed a circle around the two fallen men.

"Are you all right, Mike?" Surgenor breathed, discovering that although he was unable to move he still had the power of speech.

"I'm just great," Targett said bitterly. "Welcome with open arms, you said. That's the last time I'll take your advice about any . . ."

"Be silent, you devil creatures!" One of the near-naked captors, a heavily muscled man with black hair, raised his spear threateningly and moved closer to Targett.

"Don't harm him, Chack," said another of the group in a commanding voice. He was tall and coppery-haired, and his expression – in contrast to the hostility shown by his companions – was one of intense curiosity.

"Have you gone mad, Harld? This is exactly what King Garadan told us might happen some day." Chack pointed accusingly at Surgenor and Targett. "He prophesied that devils in human form might invade our valley and destroy us and all our families."

"Two isn't much of an invasion force – and how can they

destroy us while they are paralysed by the juice of the carpal plant?" The puzzlement in Harld's brown eyes deepened as he looked down at the two captives. "These seem more like ordinary men than . . ."

Chack sneered. "The devils are *pretending* to be human to catch us off guard, just as the King warned. I say we should kill the monsters now." There was a rumble of approval from others in the group.

"Listen to me," Surgénor said urgently, fixing his gaze on the man called Harld. "We *are* ordinary men, just like you. The fact that we speak the same language proves it. We came to this world in a starship – just as you or your ancestors must have done . . ."

"Lies!" Chack bellowed. "There is only one language, and all must speak it. Our people have always lived here, and these creatures couldn't have come from the sky, because the moons and the stars are all controlled by King Garadan. The devils are trying to confuse us – I say we have to finish them now."

Several of the group started forward, raising their spears, but they drew back when Harld leaped into the centre of the circle. "I am the leader of this hunting party, and I will decide what must be done."

"We await your decision, great leader," a third man said sarcastically.

"I . . ." Harld gazed uncertainly at Surgenor and Targett. "Bind their hands. We will take them to the King."

Two of the group immediately took cords from their waist pouches, knelt down and tied the captives' wrists together behind their backs. Surgenor was relieved to find that the paralysing weakness was beginning to leave his limbs, but there was little comfort in the discovery. It appeared that the little colony of shipwreck survivors on Korrill IV had been there long enough, perhaps well over a hundred years, to have forgotten all about their origins and to have degenerated into barbarism. And he did not look forward to meeting Garadan, their so-called king, who seemed to rule through superstition, fear and cruelty.

Several of the men raised Surgenor and Targett to their feet, laughing at the way in which they staggered and swayed on drug-weakened legs, then the entire group moved off down the slope. It was already growing dusk in the narrow valley and the racing varicoloured moons visibly changed position overhead, but Surgenor could not appreciate the eerie beauty of the scene. The green valley which had looked so enticing at first sight was now filled with menace, the promise of death.

"There's one good thing," Targett whispered as he stumbled along at Surgenor's side. "They didn't take our ultralasers – they mustn't have recognised them as weapons."

"I doubt if that's going to make much difference," Surgenor replied. "The characters who tied us up knew what they were doing. My hands are numb already."

"Does that mean we've nothing going for us at all?"

"I wouldn't say that. I took the precaution of wearing a communicorder – so Aesop can see and hear everything that's happening to us."

"Are you sure it's working?" Targett glanced doubtfully at the button-like device on Surgenor's lapel. "Aesop hasn't said anything."

"That's because he isn't stupid," Surgenor said. "How long would we last in this company with a ghost voice? You can take it that Aesop knows what's going on."

"I don't see what difference that makes," Targett replied gloomily. "He can't bring the ship down here because of all those damned moons, and he can't use heavy weaponry from orbit without vaporising us as well."

"We'll have to trust Aesop to come up with something – that's his job." Surgenor tried to sound optimistic, concealing his unease at having to trust his life to the resourcefulness of a distant and artificial intelligence. It was a situation which had occurred more than once during his years in the Cartographical Service, but he was never going to get used to it.

"Aesop? Who is this Aesop you speak of?" The voice was that of Farld, who had moved closer to Surgenor as they negotiated a bend in the tricky downwards path.

Surgenor decided against trying to explain that Aesop was an intelligent machine. "He is the captain of our starship."

Harld glanced around, making sure he was not overheard. "Just before he died my father told me a strange story. He said our people had come to this valley in a ship which fell from the sky. He warned me not to repeat the story, because the King would be angry. I thought nothing more of it until I heard you talk of similar things, then I began to wonder . . ."

"We told you the truth," Surgenor whispered. "We're not devils. We are men and we can help your people. We can bring you food and clothing and medicine. You must let us return to our ship."

Harld shook his head. "I dare not go against King Garadan. He is all-seeing and all-powerful."

"He is only a man. We can protect you from him."

"Nobody can do that," Harld said. "Why, the very moons in the sky do as he bids them."

"What do you mean?"

Harld glanced up at the narrowing strip of sky. "If the King commands a green moon to cross above us it will do so. His power and his magic extend to the heavens. I dare not challenge him lest he summons the Blood Moon." As though fearful of having said too much, Harld moved away and rejoined the other hunters.

"What do you make of all that?" Surgenor said to Targett.

"There was the same kind of set-up in some primitive societies back on Earth," Targett replied. "Priests who learned some astronomy were able to terrorise ordinary folk by appearing to order eclipses to happen."

"So this King Garadan knows the planet's moon system pretty well. What's so impressive about that? Other people must have noticed recurring cycles and patterns of . . ."

"That's just it, Dave," Targett said grimly. "There aren't any regular cycles. This planet has so many moons, all jostling and tugging at each other – especially the forty-three major ones – that the pattern never repeats. If this King Garadan can predict astronomical events on this planet he must be a genius. I don't like the sound of him, Dave – and I'll tell you something I like even less."

"What's that?"

"On the way into this system we observed that one of the largest moons had a lot of iron oxides on the surface, giving it a deep red colour. That must be the one they call the Blood Moon – and I've got a funny feeling they weren't just being poetical when they chose that name."

The village consisted of perhaps fifty small huts made of mud and straw. The mean dwellings were arranged in a double line along the narrow floor of the valley, and men, women and children – most of them looking under-nourished – had gathered to watch the arrival of the two captive devils. As Surgenor and Targett were herded by, the people clustered behind and followed them. In a very short time they reached a much larger building which, in spite of the increasing darkness, glowed with the lustre of polished metal.

"It's built out of hull plates from a spaceship," Targett whispered. "That must be where Garadan lives."

"And he's coming out to welcome us in person," Surgenor replied, his eyes intent on the figure of a middle-aged man who was emerging from the metal building. King Garadan was, in contrast to his subjects, dressed in a richly textured robe. He carried a small carved box which seemed to be inlaid with gold and gems. His body looked plump and soft, but there was nothing soft about his eyes. He regarded Surgenor and Targett with cold hostility for a few seconds, then turned to Harld.

"Why did you bring the devils here?" he demanded. "My orders have always been clear. You should have killed them before they had any chance to bring harm to my people."

Harld took a deep breath. "Sire, they seem more like men than devils."

"That is part of their devilish trickery."

"But if they are so powerful and dangerous, why do they need to employ trickery? And why was it so easy for us to capture them if . . ?"

"Silence!" Garadan's face was pale with anger. "Do you question my divine authority?"

"No, Sire." Harld glanced at the watchful circle of villagers. "But our food grows scarce and some of our children will die in the coming winter. The strangers said they could give us food and clothing. I thought it would be better if . . ."

"You presumed to know better than your King!" Garadan stared coldly at the villagers, some of whom had begun to whisper among themselves on hearing Harld speak of food and clothing. They shuffled their feet uneasily and lowered their heads.

"Don't be alarmed," Garadan said to them. "The gods grow angry, but not at you. It is Harld who has earned their wrath by bringing the devils here and sowing doubt in your minds." Garadan glanced down at his ornately carved box. "As a portent of their anger – and of my divine authority – they are sending four white moons. The light from the moons will turn night in the valley into day, to remind you that the gods can see into your innermost thoughts and will punish the unfaithful.

"The moons will appear . . ." Garadan again glanced into the box he carried. ". . . now!"

Garadan pointed upwards at the eastern rim of the valley, and there was a gasp from the assembly as the brilliant white disk of a large moon appeared, closely followed by three others. For a minute the valley was brightly illuminated by the four speeding satellites, then they had crossed the visible strip of sky and near-darkness returned. There was a hushed silence.

"The King is all-powerful," a woman cried in a thin, wailing voice. "We must obey him and kill the devils."

"That is your only way to appease the gods," Garadan shouted in a voice which was hoarse with triumph. "Prepare the devils for execution. I have commanded the Blood Moon to appear in a short time – and the devils must die as soon as its light falls on the altar."

The altar was a flat circular stone close to the entrance of Garadan's metal palace. It was ringed by flickering torches whose light gleamed irregularly on the massive two-edged sword which waited on a gilded trestle. Surgenor and Targett, bound hand and foot, had been laid down beside each other in the centre of the rock. The entire population of the village was gathered around the altar, watching and waiting.

"At least we now know how Garadan does it," Surgenor said to his younger companion. "One of his ancestors must have salvaged a small computer from the wreck of their ship, and his family has been using it ever since to overawe all the others with their so-called divine powers. It's a neat set-up Garadan has here – living in luxury with hundreds of abject slaves."

"I thought Harld was beginning to get through to them when he mentioned food and clothing," Targett said. "But you have to hand it to Garadan – he made good use of those four white moons coming along when they did."

"It's what he's going to do when the red moon appears that bothers me." Surgenor made another futile attempt to loosen his bonds. "How long do you think we've got?"

"Who knows? Maybe a couple of hours."

A dark coldness gathered inside Surgenor as he considered the idea that all of Earth's vaunted technology was powerless to save them from death at the hands of a pitiful group of primitives. "Hear these words, Aesop," he said bitterly, addressing himself via his communicorder button to the computer on board his ship. "Where are you? What are you *doing* up there?"

"There's nothing Aesop *can* do," Targett said, with a gloomy fatalism. "It may be days before he can get the *Sarafand* down through that screen of satellites, and by that time it will be all over."

"He must have told the other modules to change course and get here."

"Yes, but that won't make any difference either. Even the nearest modules couldn't possibly reach us until . . ." Targett's words were lost in a sudden hubbub of excitement from the crowd.

Surgenor turned his head and saw that the robed figure of Garadan had appeared at the entrance of his palace. Still carrying his carved and bejewelled box, Garadan walked slowly towards the altar and the villagers parted to make way for him. In the flickering light of the torches his face was immobile and inhuman as he reached the edge of the flat rock and stepped up on to it. He raised one hand imperiously and an expectant silence descended over the crowd.

"The Blood Moon answers my command," Garadan proclaimed in ringing tones. "Soon it will appear above you – to oversee and sanctify the execution of the devil creatures."

"You won't get away with this, Garadan," Surgenor said fiercely, struggling with his bonds. "We're not alone on this world. Our friends are on their way to us right now . . . with powerful weapons . . ."

"The devils are trying even more of their lies and trickery," Garadan said, glancing down into his box. "But nothing can save them because . . ." He raised his right hand and pointed upwards at the eastern edge of the strip of sky. "I command the Blood Moon to appear . . . NOW!"

A dreadful fascination drew Surgenor's gaze to the rim of the valley. His heart began a frenzied pounding as he waited for the emergence of the first sliver of crimson brightness which would herald the end of his life. And in the midst of all his fears and regrets was one persistent, pounding question: *Why had Aesop not even tried to help them?*

The silence overhanging the strange scene was absolute. Every eye was fixed on the designated portion of the sky.

Surgenor had endured the suspense for perhaps twenty seconds, perhaps thirty – time had ceased to have any meaning for him – when he began to realise that Garadan's computer had been slightly out in its prediction. The red satellite was taking longer to show up than expected. The watching villagers must have thought the delay unusual because they began to stir a little.

Garadan put his hand into the carved box, obviously interrogating the computer inside. "The Blood Moon will appear," he shouted, but now there was an edge of panic in his voice. "I, King Garadan, hav ordered it so."

More drawn-out seconds dragged by as the sky remained dark, and there was an increasingly restless murmuring from the crowd. Surgenor began to feel a flickering of hope. Something had definitely gone wrong with the computer prediction, and therein lay his and Targett's chance of salvation.

"The Blood Moon refuses to appear," he called out. "The gods have turned against Garadan! It is a sign they want us set free."

"Be silent!" Garadan snarled. "All of you, be silent! I am your king and I command you to . . ."

"He's just an ordinary man," Surgenor cut in, raising his voice against the growing clamour among the watchers. "One who has been tricking you into serving him while your children go cold and hungry. Don't be fooled any longer. This is your chance to . . ."

Surgenor's voice faded as Garadan, with a growl of hatred, dropped his box and ran to the trestle which supported the ceremonial sword. Garadan snatched up the weapon, turned to Surgenor and raised the gleaming blade above his head. The blade had begun its downward sweep when there was a sudden movement near the edge of the altar. A hunting spear swished through the air and hit Garadan full on the chest. He fell backwards, twitched spasmodically, and then was still.

Surgenor recognised Harld's coppery hair as the hunter leaped up on to the flat rock and held up his hands to quieten the circle of villagers.

"Listen to me," Harld called out. "I have slain Garadan, and the gods did nothing to save him, which proves he was just an ordinary man – exactly as the strangers said. I believe that they too are ordinary men – not devils – and I also believe they can do much good for all of us.

"Let us at least hear what they have to say. And if, when they have done, you are not satisfied that they speak the truth – then you can put them, and me, to the sword."

During the silence that followed, Surgenor became aware of Mike Targett squirming closer to him. "You always liked to hear yourself talk, big man," Targett said, his voice quavering with relief. "Now's your chance – the stage is all yours."

*

Early on the following morning, having said a temporary goodbye to the villagers, Surgenor and Targett began the long climb to the rim of the valley. They wanted to wait in their own vehicle for the arrival of the other survey modules, and for the eventual landing of the *Sarafand*. That would be the first step in the long job of rehabilitating and educating the lost colony of humans, and ultimately of returning them to Earth.

"That was the luckiest escape we're ever likely to have," Targett said. "Do you realise that if Garadan's computer hadn't gone wrong just when it did we would be dead men?"

"I don't need to be reminded of that fact," Surgenor replied soberly. "And a fat lot of good Aesop was to us! When I get back to the ship I might take a hammer and put a few dents in his memory banks."

"I advise you not to damage official property, David." The voice issuing from Surgenor's communicorder button was unmistakably that of Aesop.

"So you're still functioning, Aesop," Surgenor said. "I was beginning to think you had developed a short circuit."

"My circuits are immune to that kind of malfunction," Aesop said pedantically. "I could not communicate with you while you were within earshot of the people in the village. As you surmised, it would have been too disturbing for them."

Surgenor snorted to show his displeasure. "We got a bit disturbed ourselves, you know. If Garadan's computer hadn't fouled up . . ."

"His computer was working perfectly," Aesop cut in. "It is a TCM 84C – a type which was widely used in colonisation ships in the last century and which is noted for great reliability. I might also add that Garadan had programmed it extremely well – he must have had a natural talent in that respect."

"But . . ." Surgenor struggled to comprehend what he was hearing. "What went wrong with his prediction about the red moon?"

"It was a simple lack of input data," Aesop said emotionless as ever. "Garadan had no way of knowing that I had decided to discredit him in the eyes of his followers in order to preserve your life and that of Michael."

"Discredit him? How?"

"By intercepting the red moon while it was still at a distant point in its orbit and detonating my entire arsenal of anti-meteor weapons on its northern hemisphere." Aesop continued speaking in matter-of-fact tones, as though discussing a minor adjustment to a coffee machine. "The deviation in the moon's path was slight, of course, but it was cumulative and sufficient to prevent it being seen from the bottom of the valley."

"Holy . . . !" Targett halted, his jaw sagging with surprise.

"So what you're telling us," Surgenor went on, "is that you calmly knocked the moon out of its orbit!"

Shocked by the magnitude of the concept, Surgenor was once again reminded of the gulf which existed between his own human mentality and that of Aesop. To a human being there was something blasphemous in changing the appearance of the very heavens to suit the needs of presumptuous men – but Aesop worked as a pure intellect, unhampered by any emotion. To Aesop a problem was simply an exercise in logic; nothing more, nothing less.

"The direct approach to a problem is often the most effective," Aesop said. "Don't you agree, David?"

"Oh, absolutely," Surgenor replied airily, striving to regain his composure. There had been a dry quality to Aesop's voice, one he had noticed on previous occasions and which had led him to wonder if Aesop could be poking fun at him. Was it possible for a computer to have a sense of humour?

Surgenor considered the notion for a moment, then he shook his head and continued climbing towards the snowfields which gleamed in the sunshine far above.

DEFLATION 2001

Having to pay ten dollars for a cup of coffee shook Lester Perry.

The price had been stabilised at eight dollars for almost a month, and he had begun to entertain an irrational hope that it would stay there. He stared sadly at the vending machine as the dark liquid gurgled into a plastic cup. His expression of gloom became more pronounced when he raised the cup to his lips.

"Ten dollars," he said. "And when you get it, it's cold!"

His pilot, Boyd Dunhill, shrugged and then examined the gold braid of his uniform in case he had marred its splendour with the unaccustomed movement of his shoulders. "What do you expect?" he replied indifferently. "The airport authorities refused the Coffee Machine Maintenance Workers' pay claim last week, so the union told its members to work to rule and that has forced up the costs."

"But they got a hundred per cent four weeks ago! That's when coffee went up to eight dollars."

"The union's original claim was for *two* hundred per cent."

"But how could the airport pay two hundred per cent, for God's sake?"

"The Chocolate Machine Workers got it," Dunhill commented.

"Did they?" Perry shook his head in bewilderment. "Was that on television?"

"There hasn't been any television for three months," the pilot reminded him. "The technicians' claim for a basic two million a year is still being disputed."

Perry drained his coffee cup and threw it in the bin. "Is my plane ready? Can we go now?"

"It's been ready for four hours."

"Then why are we hanging around here?"

"The Light Aircraft Engineers' productivity agreement – there's a statutory minimum of eight hours allowed for all maintenance jobs."

"Eight hours to replace a wiper blade!" Perry laughed shakily. "And that's a productivity deal?"

"It has doubled the number of man-hours logged at this field."

"Of course it has, if they're putting down eight hours for half-hour jobs. But that's a completely false . . ." Perry stopped speaking as he saw the growing coldness on his pilot's face. He remembered, just in time, that there was a current pay dispute between the Flying Employers Association and the Low-wing Twin-engined Private Airplane Pilots Union. The employers were offering 75% and the pilots were holding out for 150%, plus a mileage bonus. "Can you get a porter to carry my bag?"

Dunhill shook his head. "You'll have to carry it yourself. They're on strike since last Friday."

"Why?"

"Too many people were carrying their own bags."

"Oh!" Perry lifted his case and took it out across the tarmac to the waiting aircraft. He strapped himself into one of the five passenger seats, reached for a magazine to read during the flight to Denver, then recalled that there had been no newspapers or magazines for over two weeks. The preliminaries of getting airborne took an unusually long time – suggesting the air traffic controllers were engaged in some kind of collective bargaining – and finally Perry drifted into an uneasy sleep.

He was shocked into wakefulness by a sound of rushing air which told him the door of the aircraft had been opened in flight. Physically and mentally chilled, he opened his eyes and saw Dunhill standing at the yawning door. His expensive uniform was pulled into peculiar shapes by the harness of a parachute.

"What . . . What is this?" Perry said. "Are we on fire?"

"No." Dunhill was using his best official voice. "I'm on strike."

"You're kidding!"

"You think so? I just got word on the radio – the employers have turned down the very reasonable demands of the Low-wing Twin-engined Private Airplane Pilots Union and walked out on the negotiations. We've got the backing of our friends in the Low-wing Single-engines and in the High-wing Twin-engines Unions, consequently all our members are withdrawing their labour at midnight, which is about thirty seconds from now."

"But, *Boyd*! I've no chute – what'll happen to me?"

A look of sullen determination appeared on the pilot's face. "Why should I worry about you? You weren't very concerned about me when I was trying to get along on a bare three million a year."

"I was selfish. I see that now, and I'm sorry." Perry unstrapped himself and stood up. "Don't jump, Boyd – I'll double your salary."

"That," Dunhill said impatiently, "is less than our union is claiming."

"Oh! Well, I'll triple it then. Three times your present salary, Boyd."

"Sorry. No piecemeal settlements. They weaken union solidarity." He turned away and dived into the roaring blackness beyond the doorway.

Perry stared after him for a moment, then wrestled the door shut and went forward to the cockpit. The aircraft was flying steadily on autopilot. Perry sat down in the left-hand seat and gripped the control column, casting his mind back several decades to his days as a fighter pilot in Vietnam. Landing the aircraft himself would get him in serious trouble with the unions for strike-breaking, but he was not prepared to die just yet. He disengaged the autopilot and began to get in some much-needed flying practice.

Some thousands of feet below the aircraft Boyd Dunhill pulled the ripcord and waited for his chute to open. The jolt, when it came, was less severe than he had expected and a few seconds later he was falling at the same speed as before. He looked upwards and saw – instead of a taut canopy – a fluttering bunch of unconnected nylon segments.

And, too late, he remembered the threat of the Parachute Stitchers and Packers Union to carry out disruptive action in support of their demand for longer vacations.

"Communists!" he screamed. "You lousy Red anarchist ba . . . ."

SHADOW OF WINGS

There was once a magician named Dardash, who – at the relatively young age of 103 – decided he had done with the world.

Accordingly, he selected an islet a short distance off the coast of Koldana and built upon it a small but comfortable house which resembled a wind-carved spire of rock. He equipped the dwelling with life's few necessities and moved into it with all his possessions – the most prized of which were twelve massive scrolls in air-tight cylinders of oiled leather bound with silver wire. He surrounded his new home with certain magical defences and, as a final touch which was intended to complete his isolation, he rendered the entire island invisible.

As has already been stated, Dardash had decided he was finished with the world.

But the world was far from being finished with him . . .

It was a flawless morning in early summer, one on which the universe seemed to have been created anew. The land to the east shimmered like freshly smelted gold, deckled with white fire where the sun's rays grazed slopes of sand; and on all other sides the flat blue immensity of the sea challenged Dardash's knowledge of history with its sheer ringing emptiness. It was as though Minoa and Egypt and Sumer had never existed, or had vanished as completely as the ancient magic-based civilisations which had preceded them. The very air sang a song of new beginnings.

Dardash walked slowly on the perimeter of his island, remembering a time when such mornings had filled him with a near-painful joy. It was a time that was lost to him.

Being a magician, he retained a long-muscled and sinewy physique which – except for its lack of scars – resembled that of a superbly conditioned warrior, but his mind was growing old, corrupted by doubt. When the twelve scrolls had first come into his possession, and he had realised they contained spells written in the mana-rich, dawn-time of magic, he had known with a fierce certainty that he was destined to become the greatest warlock that had ever lived. But that had been almost two-score years ago, and he was no longer so confident. In truth, although he rarely admitted it to himself, he had begun to despair – and all because of a single, maddening, insuperable problem.

He reached the north-eastern tip of the islet, moody and abstracted in spite of the vitality all around him, and was turning southwards when his attention was caught by a flickering whiteness at the far side of the strip of water separating him from the mainland. The coast of Koldana was rocky in that area, a good feeding ground for gulls, but the object he had noticed was too large to be a bird. It was possibly a man in white garments, although travellers were rare in that region. Dardash stared at the brilliant speck for a moment, trying to bring it into sharp focus, but even his keen eyesight was defeated by the slight blurring effect caused by the islet's invisibility screen.

He shrugged and continued his morning walk, returning his thoughts to more weighty considerations. As a man who had travelled the length and breadth of the known world, he could speak every major language and was familiar with the written forms where they existed. The fact that the spells of the twelve scrolls were couched in the Old Language had at first seemed a minor inconvenience, especially for one who was accustomed to deciphering all manner of strange inscriptions. A few months, possibly even a few years, of study would surely reveal the secrets of the old manuscripts – thus enabling him to fulfil his every dream, to become immortal, to assume all the fantastic powers of the dream-time sorcerers.

But he had not allowed for the effect of the 10,000-year hiatus.

The old magic-based civilisations – so powerful in the days when mana was plentiful everywhere – had in fact been edifices of great fragility; and when the raw stuff of magic had disappeared from the earth they too had crumbled and faded into nothingness. Few relics remained, and those that Dardash had seen or thought he had seen were totally without relevance to his quest. He lacked the necessary key to the Old Language, and as long as it remained impenetrable to him he would fail to develop anything like his full potential. The doors of destiny would remain shut against him, even though there were places where mana had again begun to accumulate, and that had been the principal reason for his retreat from outside distraction. He had elected to devote all his time, all his mental energies, all his scholarship to one supremely important task – solving the riddle of the scrolls.

Thus preoccupied, and secure behind his magical defences, Dardash should have been oblivious to the world beyond, but he had been oddly restless and lacking in concentration for some time. His mind had developed an annoying tendency to pursue the irrelevant and the trivial, and as he neared the southern corner of the island – where his house was located – he again found himself speculating about who or what had appeared on the opposite shore. Yielding to impulse, he glanced to the east and saw that the enigmatic white mote was still visible at the water's edge. He frowned at it for a short period, hesitating, then acknowledged to himself that he would have no mental peace until the inconsequential little mystery was solved.

Shaking his head at his own foolishness, he went into his house and climbed the stone stair to the upper balcony. He had used the spy-mask only the previous day to observe a ship which had appeared briefly on the western horizon, and it was still lying on the low bench, resembling the severed head of a giant eagle. Dardash fastened the mask over his face and turned towards the mainland. Because the spy-mask operated on magical and not optical principles, there was no focusing or scanning to be done – Dardash immediately saw the mysterious object on the coast as though from a distance of a few paces. And he was unable to withhold an exclamation.

The young woman was possibly the most beautiful he had ever seen. She appeared to be of Amorite stock, with the lush black hair and immaculate tawny skin of her race. Her face was that of the perfect lover that all men recognise from dreams, but which few aspire to touch in reality – dark-eyed and full-lipped, sensuous and wilful, generous yet demanding. She was standing ankle-deep in the waters of a narrow cove – a place where she could presume to remain unobserved – and, as Dardash watched, she unbuttoned her white linen chiton, cast the garment behind her on to the sand, and began to bathe.

Her movements were graceful and languorous, like those of a dance that was being performed for his sole benefit, and his mouth went dry as he took in every detail of her body, followed the course of every runnel of water from splendid breast to belly and slim-coned thigh.

Dardash had no clear idea of how long her toilet lasted. He remained in a timeless, trance-like state until she had left the water, clothed herself and was gliding away into the rocky outcrop that formed a natural palisade between sea and land. Only when she was lost to his view did he move again. He removed the eagle-mask from his head, and when he surveyed his little domain with normal vision it seemed strangely bleak and cheerless.

As he descended the stair to the principal chamber in which he did most of his work, there came to Dardash a belated understanding of his recent lack-lustre moods, of his irritability and lapses of concentration. The decision to devote his entire life to the riddle of the scrolls had been an intellectual one, but he was a composite being – a synthesis of mind and body – and the physical part of him was in rebellion. He should have brought one or more girls from an inland village when he had set up his offshore retreat a year earlier. Many would have been glad to accompany and serve him in exchange for a little basic tutelage in magic, but he had an uneasy feeling it was too late to come to such an arrangement. The women, even the youngest, of the region tended to be a sun-withered, work-hardened lot – and he had just seen the sort of companion he truly craved.

But who was she? Where had she come from, and what was her destination?

The questions troubled Dardash at intervals for the rest of the day, distracting him from the endless task of trying to relate the phonetic writing of the scrolls to the complex abstractions of his profession. It was rare for trade caravans plying between the capital city of Koldana and the northern lands to take the longer coastal route, so she was unlikely to be the daughter or concubine of a wealthy merchant. But what possibilities remained? Only in fables did princesses or others of high birth go wandering in search of knowledge. Reconciling himself to the fact that speculation was futile, Dardash worked until long after nightfall, but in spite of being weary he found it difficult to sleep. His rest was disturbed by visions of the unknown woman, and each time he awoke with the taste of her lips fading from his the sense of loss was greater, more insistent.

Part of his mood was occasioned by a belief that important opportunities only come once, that the penalty for failing to take action is eternal regret. Hence it was with a sense of near-disbelief, of having been specially favoured by the gods, that on the following morning as he walked the eastern boundary of his island he again saw the flicker of whiteness on the mainland. This time, vision aided by memory, he had no trouble interpreting the lazy pulsations and shape changes of the blurred speck. *She* was there again. Undressing, uncovering that splendid body, preening herself, preparing for the sea's caress.

Dardash paused only long enough to unfasten his sandals. He stepped down into the clear water and swam towards the mainland, propelling himself with powerful and economical strokes which quickly reduced the distance to the shore. As he passed through the perimeter of the invisibility screen which protected his islet, he saw the outline of the woman become diamond-sharp in his vision and he knew that from that moment on she would be able to see him. Apparently, however, she was too preoccupied.

It was not until Dardash felt pebbles beneath his hands and stood up, his near-naked body only knee-deep in water, that she became aware of his presence. She froze in the act of unbuttoning her chiton, breasts partly exposed, and gave him a level stare which signalled surprise and anger, but – he was thrilled to note – no hint of fear.

"I had presumed myself alone," she said coldly, her beautiful face queenly in displeasure. "Suddenly the very sea is crowded."

"There is no crowd," Dardash replied, courting her with his smile. "Only the two of us."

"Soon there will only be you." The woman turned, picked up the net pouch which contained her toiletries, and strode away from him towards the narrow entrance to the cove. Sunlight piercing the fine material of her clothing outlined her body and limbs, striking fire behind Dardash's eyes.

"Wait," he said, deciding that a challenge could be the most effective way of capturing her interest. "Surely you are not afraid?"

The woman gave a barely perceptible toss of her head and continued walking, beginning to move out of sight behind outcroppings of rock. Impelled by a growing sense of urgency, Dardash went after her with long strides, convinced that were he to fail this time he would never again have a night's peace. He had almost reached the woman, was breathing the scent of her waist-length black hair, when an inner voice warned him that he was behaving foolishly. He halted, turned to check a deep cleft in the rocks to his left, and groaned as he realised he was much too late.

The braided leather whip whistled like a war arrow as it flailed through the air, catching him just above the elbow, instantaneously binding his arms to his sides.

Dardash reacted by continuing his turn, intending to coil the whip further around his body and thus snatch it from its user's grasp, but there was a flurry of footsteps and a glint of sunlight on armour and the weight of a man hit behind the knees, bringing him down. Other armed men, moving with practised speed, dropped on top of him and he felt thongs tighten around his wrists and ankles. Within the space of three heartbeats he was immobile and helpless, and sick with anger at having allowed himself to be trapped so easily.

Narrowing his eyes against the glare from the sky, he looked up at his captors. There were four men wearing conical helmets and studded leather cuirasses. They did not look like soldiers, but the similarity of their equipment suggested they were in the employ of a person of wealth. A fifth figure – that of the woman –

joined them, causing Dardash to turn his face away. He had no wish to see a look of triumph or contempt on her face, and in any case his mind was busy with the question of who had instigated the attack against him. In his earlier years he had made many enemies, but most of them had long since died, and latterly he had devoted so much time to his scrolls that there had scarcely been the chance to incur the wrath of anybody who mattered.

"Tell me the name of your master," he said, making himself sound patient and only mildly interested. He wanted to give the impression that he was unconcerned about his safety, that he was holding tremendous magical powers in reserve, although he was actually quite helpless. Most magic required protracted and painstaking preparation, and the ruffians standing over him could easily end his life at any moment if they so desired.

"You'll find out soon enough," the tallest man said. He had a reddish stubble of a beard and one of his nostrils had been excised by an old wound that had left a diagonal scar on his face.

"You owe him no loyalty," Dardash said, experimenting with the possibilities of his situation. "By sending you against me he has placed you in terrible danger."

Red-beard laughed comfortably. "I must be a braver man than I realised – I feel absolutely no fear."

You will, Dardash vowed inwardly. *If I get out of this alive*. The sobering realisation that this could be the last day of his life caused him to lapse into a brooding silence while the four men brought a wooden litter from its place of concealment behind nearby rocks. They rolled him on to it, none too gently, and carried him up the steep slope to the higher ground of the plain that spanned most of Koldana. The woman, now more normally clad in an all-enveloping burnous, led the way. Dardash, still trying to guess why he had been taken, derived little comfort from the fact that his captors had not run a sword through him as soon as they had the chance. Their master, if he was an enemy worth considering, would want to dispose of him in person – and quite possibly by some means that would give all concerned plenty of time to appreciate what was happening.

When the party reached level ground Dardash craned his

neck, expecting to see some kind of conveyance that would be used to transport him inland, but instead there was a square tent only a few hundred paces away, positioned just far enough from the shore to be invisible from his inlet home. The tent had an awning supported on gilded poles, and near it perhaps a dozen horses and pack animals cropped the sparse vegetation. It was obviously a temporary camp set up by a personage of some importance, one who was not prepared to travel far without the trappings of luxury, and it came to Dardash that he would not be kept in ignorance of his fate much longer. He lay back on the litter and feigned indifference.

The woman ran on ahead of the others, presumably to announce their arrival, and when the group of men reached the tent she was holding the entrance flaps aside for them. They carried Dardash into the lemon-coloured shade within, set the litter down and left without speaking, closing the entrance behind them. Dardash, his eyes rapidly adjusting to the change of lighting, saw that he was alone with a plump, heavily-moustached man whose skin was as smooth and well-oiled as that of a young concubine. He was dressed in costly silks, and Dardash noted with a quickening of interest – and hope – that astrological symbols were woven into the dark blue of his robe. In Dardash's experience, astrologers were rarely men of violence – except of course towards those who made their predictions go wrong, and he was quite certain he had not done anything along those lines.

"I am Urtarra, astrologer at the court of King Marcurades," the man said. "I am sorry at having brought you here by such devious means, but . . ."

"Devious!" Dardash snorted his contempt. "It was the simplest and most childish trick ever devised."

"Nevertheless, it worked." Urtarra paused to let the implication of his words sink in. "I do hope that doesn't mean that you are simple and childish, because if you are you will be unequal to the task I have in mind for you."

"You'll learn how childish I am," Dardash promised, his anger growing apace with his new certainty that he was not about to be slain. "You'll learn a great deal about me as soon as I am free of these bonds."

Urtarra shook his head. "I have already learned all I need to know about you, and I would not be stupid enough to release you until you had heard my proposal and agreed to work for me." He eyed Dardash's robust frame. "You look as though you would wreak considerable damage, even without magical aids."

Dardash almost gasped aloud at the extent of the other man's presumption. "I don't know what miserable little desires you harbour, but I can tell you one thing – I will never serve you in any way."

"Ah, but you *will*!" Urtarra looked amused as he rearranged the cushions on which he was seated. "The fact of the matter is that I have certain unusual talents, powers which are related to your own in a way. I am a seer. I have the gift of being able to part the veils of time and divine something of what the future holds in store – and I have seen the two of us making a journey together."

"A seer?" Dardash glanced at the planetary symbols on Urtarra's robes. "I don't regard fiddling with abacus and astrolabe as . . ."

"Nor do I, but young King Marcurades does not believe in any form of magic, not even my modest variety. He is a philosopher, you must understand – one of that breed of men who put their faith in irrigation schemes rather than weather spells, armour rather than amulets. It would be impossible for me to remain at his court were I to use my powers openly. Instead, I must pretend that my predictions spring from the science of astrology. I have nothing against astrology, of course, except that it lacks . . . um . . . precision."

"Your own visions are similarly lacking," Dardash said with emphasis. "I have no intention of making any journey with you, nor will I serve you in any . . . What sort of chore did you have in mind, anyway? The usual unimaginative trivia? Preparing a love potion? Turning useful lead into useless gold?"

"No, no, no – something much more appropiate to a magician of your standing." Urtarra paused to stare into Dardash's face, and when he spoke again his voice was low and earnest. "I want you to kill King Marcurades."

Dardash's immediate and instinctive response was to begin a new struggle to break free of his bonds. He writhed and quivered on the litter, straining to loosen or snap his restraints, but the thongs were stout and had been expertly tied, and even his unusual strength was of no avail. Finally he lapsed into immobility, sweating, his gaze fixed on the roof of the tent.

"Why exhaust yourself?" Urtarra said reasonably. "Does the life of the king mean so much to you?"

"My concern is for my own life," Dardash replied. He had scant regard for rank – a prince had no more standing in his scheme of things than a pot-mender – but the young King Marcurades was a rare phenomenon in that he was a ruler who was universally admired by his subjects. In the five years since he had ascended to the throne of Koldana, Marcurades had secured the country's boundaries, expanded its trade, abolished taxes, and devoted himself to far-sighted schemes for the improvement of agriculture and industry. Under his aegis the populace were experiencing stability and prosperity to an unprecedented degree, and in return they were fiercely loyal, from the most illustrious general right down to the humblest farmworker. Dardash found it difficult to conceive of a project more foolhardy than the proposed assassination of such a king.

"Admittedly, no ordinary man could undertake the task and hope to live," Urtarra said, accurately divining Dardash's thoughts, "but you are no ordinary man."

"Nor do I take heed of flattery. Why do you wish the king dead? Are you in league with his heirs?"

"I am acting only for myself – and the people of Koldana. Let me show you something." Urtarra raised one hand and pointed at a wall of the tent. The material rippled in a way that had nothing to do with the breeze from the sea, then seemed to dissolve into mist. Through swirls of opalescent vapour, Dardash saw the erect and handsome figure of a young king standing in a chariot which was being drawn through the streets of a city.

Cheering crowds pressed in on each side, with mothers holding their infants aloft to give them a better view, and maidens coming forward to strew the chariot's path with flowers.

"That is Marcurades now," Urtarra murmured, "but let us look forward and see the course which is to be followed by the river of time."

Conjured images began to appear and fade in rapid succession, compressing time, and by means of them Dardash saw the king grow older, and with the passage of the years changes occurred in his mien. He became tight-lipped and bleak-eyed, and gradually the aspect of the royal processions altered. Great numbers of soldiers marched before and behind the king, and engines of war were in evidence. The crowds who lined the routes still cheered, but few infants or maidens were to be seen, and the onlookers were noticeably shabbier of dress and thinner of face.

The prescience which Dardash was experiencing was more than simply a progression of images. Knowledge, foreknowledge, was being vouchsafed to him in wordless whispers, and he knew that the king was to be corrupted by power and ambition, to become increasingly cruel and insane. He was to raise armies and conquer neighbouring countries, thus augmenting his military might. Marcurades was to turn his back on all his enlightened reforms and civil engineering projects. Finally he was to attempt to increase his domain a thousand-fold, plunging the entire region into a series of terrible wars and catastrophes –resulting in the total annihilation of his people.

As the last dire vision faded, and the wall of the tent became nothing more than a slow-billowing square of cloth, Dardash looked at Urtarra with new respect. "You *are* a seer," he said. "You have a gift which even I can only envy."

"Gift? Curse is a better word for it." For an instant Urtarra's smooth face looked haunted. "I could well do without such visions and the burden of responsibility they bring."

"What burden? Now that you know what is preordained for Koldana and its people, all you have to do is journey to some safe country and live out your life in peace. That's what I'm going to do."

"But I am not you," Urtarra said. "And the events we saw are not preordained. Time is like a river, and the course of a river can be altered – that's why you must kill the king before it is too late."

Dardash settled back on the litter. "I have no intention of involving myself in anything so troublesome and dangerous. Why should I?"

"But you have just *seen* the miseries that are held in store for multitudes – the wars and plagues and famines."

"What's that to me?" Dardash said casually. "I have my own problems to contend with, and very little time in which to do it. I'll make you an offer – you release me now and I will promise to go my separate way without harming you or any of your company."

"I was told you thought only of yourself," Urtarra said, his eyes mirroring a cynical amusement, "but it was hard to believe a man could be so lacking in compassion."

"Believe it." Dardash proffered his bound wrists. "Let's get this over with no more waste of time."

"There is one thing you have not considered," Urtarra said, his voice oddly enigmatic as he rose to his feet and walked to a richly ornamented chest which sat in one corner of the tent. "I am willing to repay you for your services."

Dardash gave a humourless laugh. "With what? Gold or precious stones? I can conjure them out of dung! The favours of that whore who lingers outside? I can recruit a hundred like her in any city. You have nothing which could possibly interest me, soothsayer."

"That is most regrettable," Urtarra said mildly as he stooped and took something from the chest. "I hoped you might find something worthy of your attention in this."

He turned and Dardash saw that he was holding a piece of parchment, roughly two handsbreadths in length, which had obviously been cut from a scroll. Dardash gave the parchment a bored glance and was turning his head away again when there came a thrill of recognition – it bore lines of writing in the Old Language, the same enigmatic and impenetrable script of his own twelve scrolls. Apart from the compilations of spells which had defeated his understanding for decades, no other matter written in the Old Langauge had come his way. Dardash tilted his head for a better view, trying to decide what kind of text the fragment represented, and suddenly – as though he had been stricken by a superior magic – he was unable to speak or breathe. His heartbeat became a tumult of thunder within his chest and bright-haloed specks danced across his vision as he absorbed the realisation that the parchment in Urtarra's hands was written in *two* languages.

Under each line of the Old Language was a corresponding line, a mixture of ideograms and phonetic symbols, which Dardash identified as late period Accosian – one of the near-defunct languages he had mastered many years earlier.

"This is only a fragment, of course," Urtarra said. "I have the remainder of the scroll hidden in a secure place, but if it's of no interest to you . . ."

"Don't toy with me – I don't like it." Dardash briefly considered the fact that the key which would unlock the secrets of his twelve scrolls would make him virtually immortal, with all the incredible powers of the ancient warlocks, and decided he should modify his attitude towards Urtarra. "I admit to having a certain scholarly interest in old writings, and am prepared to offer a fair price for good examples. The assassination of a king is out of the question, of course, but there are many other . . ."

"And don't you toy with me," Urtarra cut in. "Marcurades has to die – otherwise the entire scroll will be consigned to the fire."

The threat cast a chill shadow in Dardash's mind.

"On the other hand, the world has seen an abundance of kings," he said slowly. "Is it a matter of any real consequence whether we have one more – or one less?"

It was close to noon by the time Dardash had selected the magical equipment he thought he would need and had brought it ashore by raft. He supervised the loading of the material and some personal effects on to two mules, then turned to Urtarra with a slight frown.

"Just to satisfy my curiosity," he said, "how were you able to find my unobtrusive little island? I believed I had it quite well concealed."

"It was *very* well concealed – from the eyes of men," Urtarra replied, allowing himself to look satisfied. "But birds can see it from on high, and you have many of them nesting there."

"What difference does that make?"

"To me – none; to the hawks I have been releasing – a great deal."

"I see," Dardash said thoughtfully, suddenly aware that Urtarra, for all his eunuchoid softness, would make a highly dangerous adversary. "Have you ever thought of becoming a sorcerer?"

"Never! I'm troubled enough by visions as it is. Were I to introduce new elements I might forfeit sleep altogether."

"Perhaps you're right." Dardash swung himself up into the saddle of the horse that had been provided for him. "Tell me, do you ever foresee your own death?"

"No seer can do that – not until he is ready." Urtarra gave him an odd smile and made a signal to his four guards and the young woman, all of whom were already on horseback and waiting some distance away. They moved off immediately, taking a south-easterly course for Bhitsala, the capital city of Koldana. The plain was shimmering with heat and at the horizon there was no clear distinction between land and sky.

Dardash, who much preferred the comparative coolness of the coast, had no relish for the four days' ride that lay ahead. Urging his horse forward alongside Urtarra, he consoled himself with the thought that this journey was probably the last he would have to undertake in such a commonplace and uncomfortable manner. When the knowledge reposing in the twelve scrolls was available to him he would waft himself effortlessly to his destinations by other means, perhaps sailing on clouds, perhaps by methods as yet undreamed of. Until then he would have to make the best of things as they were.

"The woman," he said pensively, "has she any knowledge of what we're about?"

"None! Nobody else must learn what has passed between us – otherwise your power and mine increased a hundredfold couldn't preserve our lives."

"Don't your men regard this expedition as being a little . . . unusual?"

"They are trained never to ask nor to answer questions. However, I have told them what I will tell Marcurades – that you are a superb mathematician, and that I need your help in calculating horoscopes. I have spread word that the stars are hinting at some major event, but are doing it in such an obscure way that even I am baffled. It all helps to prepare the ground."

Dardash's thoughts returned to the female figure ahead. "And where did you obtain the woman?"

"Nirrineen is the daughter of one of my cousins." Urtarra gave a satisfied chuckle. "It was fortunate that she was so well qualified for the task I assigned her. Shall I send her to you tonight?"

"That won't be necessary," Dardash said, concealing his annoyance at what he regarded as an insult. "She will come to me of her own accord."

The group trekked across the acrid plain – seemingly at the centre of a hazy hemisphere of blinding radiance – until, with the lowering of the sun, the horizons became sharp again, and the world was created anew all around them. In the period of tranquillity that preceded nightfall they set up camp – the stately square tent for Urtarra's sole usage, humbler conical structures for the others – and fires were lit. Nirrineen began to prepare a meal for Urtarra and Dardash, leaving the four guards to cater for their own needs. Dardash chose to stand close to the young woman while she worked, placing her within the orbit of a personal power which was slow-acting but sure.

"You were excellent when we met this morning," he said. "I quite believed you were a princess."

"And I quite believe you are a flatterer." Nirrineen did not raise her eyes from the dishes she was preparing.

"I never employ flattery."

"It exists most in its denial."

"Very good," Dardash said, chuckling, his desire quickening as he realised that the woman kneeling before him was a complete person and not merely a shell of flesh. "Yesterday, when I watched you bathe, I knew . . ."

"Yesterday?" Her eyes glimmered briefly in the dusk, like twin moons.

"Yes. Don't forget that I'm as much magician as mathematician. Yesterday – by proxy – I stood very close to you for a long time, and knew then that you and I had been fashioned for each other. Like sword and sheath."

"Sword! Can it be that you now flatter yourself?"

"There's but one way for you to find out," Dardash replied easily. Much later as they lay together in the darkness, with Nirrineen contentedly asleep in his arms, he exulted in the discovery that his mind had regained all of its former clarity.

He began to consider ways of killing the king.

The city of Bhitsala was clustered around a semi-circular bay which provided good anchorage for trading ships. It was protected by a range of low hills which merged with the shoreline at the bay's southern edge, creating a cliff-edge prominence upon which sat the palace of the Koldanian kings. It was a sprawling, multi-centred building, the colonnades of which had been sheathed with beaten gold until Marcurades' accession to the throne. One of the young king's first actions after assuming power had been to strip the columns and distribute the gold among his people. The under-lying cores of white marble shone almost as brightly, however, and at the end of the day when they reflected the aureate light of sunset the dwellers in the city below told their children that the gods had gilded the palace anew to repay Marcurades for his generosity.

Dardash imagined he could sense the universal adoration of the king as he rode into the city, and for him it was an atmosphere of danger. The task he had undertaken would have to be planned and carried out with the utmost care. He had already decided that it must not appear to be a murder at all, but even a naturally occurring illness could lead to suspicions of poisoning – and a magician, a reputed brewer of strange potions and philtres, was one of the most likely to be accused. It was essential, Dardash told himself, that Marcurades' death should occur in public, before as many witnesses as possible, and that it should appear as either a pure accident or, even better, a malign stroke of fate. The trouble was that divine acts were difficult to simulate.

"I have prepared a room for you in my own quarters at the palace," Urtarra said as they passed through the city's afternoon heat and began the gradual climb to the royal residence. "You will be able to rest there and have a meal."

"That's good," Dardash replied, "but first I'm going to bathe and have Nirrineen massage me with scented oils – I've begun to smell worse than this accursed horse."

"My intention was to send Nirrineen straight back to her father."

"No! I want her to stay with me."

"But many women are available at the palace." Urtarra brought his horse closer and lowered his voice. "It wouldn't be wise at this time to share your bed with one who has a special interest in you."

Dardash realised at once that Urtarra's counsel was good, but the thought of parting with Nirrineen – the she-creature who worked her own kind of voluptuous magic on him through the sweet hours of night – was oddly painful. "Don't alarm yourself – she will know nothing," he said. "Do you take me for a fool?"

"I was thinking only of your own safety."

"There is only one whose safety is at risk," Dardash said, fixing his gaze on the complex architecture of the palace which had begun to dominate the skyline ahead.

When they reached the palace gates a short time later, Urtarra conferred briefly with his men and sent them on their way to nearby lodgings. Dardash, Urtarra and Nirrineen were able to ride through the gates after only a perfunctory examination by the captain of the palace guard – yet another indication of the unusual bond that existed between the king and his subjects. Servants summoned by Urtarra led away their horses and mules. Others came forward to carry Dardash's belongings into the astrologer's suite, which was part of a high wing facing the sea, but he dismissed them and moved the well-trussed bundles in person.

While thus engaged he noticed, in one corner of a small courtyard, a strange vehicle which consisted principally of a large wooden barrel mounted on four wheels. At the base of the barrel was an arrangement of cylinders and copper pipes from which projected a long T-shaped handle, and near the top – coiled like a snake – was a flexible leather tube, the seams of which were sealed with bitumen.

"What is that device?" Dardash said, pointing the object out to Urtarra. "I've never seen its like before."

Urtarra looked amused. "You'll see many of Marcurades' inventions before you are here very long. He calls that particular one a fire engine."

"A fire engine? Is it a siege weapon?"

"Quite the opposite," Urtarra said, his amusement turning to outright laughter. "It's for projecting water on to burning buildings."

"Oh? An unusual sport for a king."

"It's more than a sport, my friend. Marcurades gets so obsessed with his various inventions that he spends half his time in the palace workshops. Sometimes, in his impatience to see the latest one completed, he throws off his robes and labours on it like a common artisan. I've seen him emerge from the smithy so covered with soot and sweat as to be almost unrecognisable."

"Doesn't he know that such activities can be dangerous?"

"Marcurades doesn't care about . . ." Urtarra paused and scanned Dardash's face. "What are you thinking?"

"I'm not sure yet." Dardash almost smiled as his mind came to grips with the information he had just received. "Now, where can I bathe?"

"Watch this," Dardash said to Nirrineen as they stood together in the elaborate garden which formed a wide margin between the royal palace and the edge of the cliffs. It was a fresh morning and the livening breeze coming in from the sea was ideally suited to

Dardash's purpose. In his right hand he had a cross made from two flat strips of hardwood, smoothly jointed at the centre. He raised his hand and made to throw the cross off the edge of the cliff.

"Don't throw it away," Nirrineen pleaded. She had no idea why Dardash had constructed the cross in the first place, but she had seen him spend the best part of a day carefully shaping the object, smoothly rounding some edges and sharpening others, and obviously she disliked the idea of his labour going to waste.

"But I've grown weary of the thing," Dardash said, laughing. He brought his hand down sharply, in an action like that of a man cracking a whip, and released the cross. It flew from his fingers at great speed, its arms flailing in the vertical plane, gradually curving downwards towards the blue waters of the bay. Nirrineen began to protest, but her voice was stilled as the cross, tilting to one side, defied gravity by sailing upwards again until it was higher than the point from which it had been launched. It appeared to come to rest in mid-air, hovering like a hawk, twinkling brightly in the sky. Nirrineen gave a small scream of mingled wonder and terror as she realised the cross was actually returning. She threw herself into Dardash's arms as the strange artifact fluttered back across the edge of the cliff and fell to earth a few paces away.

"You didn't tell me it was bewitched," she accused, clinging to Dardash and staring down at the cross as though it were a live thing which might suddenly attack her.

"There is no magic here," he said, disengaging himself and picking up the cross, "even though I learned the secret from a very old book. Look at how I have shaped each piece of wood to resemble a gull's wing. I've made you a little wooden bird, Nirrineen – a homing pigeon."

"It still seems like magic to me," she said doubtfully. "I don't think I like it."

"You soon shall. See how reluctant it is to leave you." Dardash threw the cross out to sea again in the same manner and it repeated its astonishing circular flight, this time coming to rest even closer to its starting point. Nirrineen leaped out of its path, but now there was more excitement than apprehension in her eyes, and after a third throw she was able to bring herself to pick the cross up and hand it to Dardash.

He went on throwing it, varying the speed and direction of its flight and making a game for both of them out of avoiding its whirring returns. In a short time a group of palace servants and minor officials, initially attracted by Nirrineen's laughter, had gathered to watch the spectacle. Dardash continued tirelessly, apparently oblivious to the onlookers, but in fact paying careful attention to every detail of his surroundings, and he knew – simply by detecting a change in the general noise level – the exact moment at which his plan had succeeded. He turned and saw the knot of spectators part to make way for the approach of a handsome, slightly-built young man, whose bearing somehow managed to be both relaxed and imperious.

This is a new kind of arrogance, Dardash thought. *Here is a man who feels that he doesn't even have to try to impress . . .*

The remainder of the thought was lost as he got his first direct look at the young King Marcurades and felt the ruler's sheer psychic power wash over him. Dardash, as a dedicated magician, understood very well that there was more to his calling than the willingness and ability to memorise spells. On a number of occasions he had encountered men – often in ordinary walks of life – who had a strong potential for magic, but never before had he been confronted by a human being whose charisma was so overwhelming. Dardash suddenly found himself taken aback, humbled and confused, by the realisation that he was in the company of a man who, had he been so inclined, could have effortlessly eclipsed him in his chosen profession.

"You must be Urtarra's new assistant," Marcurades said in light and pleasant tones. "I trust that you are enjoying your stay in Bhitsala."

Dardash bowed. "I'm enjoying it very much, sire – it is my privilege to serve your highness." To himself he said: *Can it, despite Urtarra's visions, be right to kill such a man?*

"I am sorry we could not meet sooner, but the demands on my time are myriad." Marcurades paused and glanced at Nirrineen. "However, I suspect you are in little need of consolation."

Nirrineen smiled and lowered her gaze in a way which, to
Dardash's heightened sensibilities, had nothing to do with
modesty. *The bitch*, he thought, appalled at the strength of his
emotion. *The bitch is ready to give herself to him, right here and
now.*

"I couldn't help observing that you cast more than horoscopes," Marcurades said, nodding at the cross which lay on the
grass nearby. "That scrap of wood appears to have magical
power, but – as I am no believer in hocus-pocus – I surmise it has
qualities of form which are not immediately apparent."

"Indeed, sire." Dardash retrieved the cross and, with murder
in his heart, began to explain what he knew of the aerodynamic
principles which made the circular flights possible. Now that his
attitude towards Marcurades had crystallised, the facts that the
king addressed him as an equal and chose to wear unadorned linen
garments were further evidence of an incredible arrogance, of an
overweening pride. It was not difficult to understand how such
attributes could decay into a terrible and dangerous insanity,
gradually corrupting the young king until he had become a
monster the world could well do without.

"As soon as the cross ceases to spin it falls to the ground,"
Dardash said. "That shows that it is the fleet movement of these
arms through the air which somehow makes the cross as light as
thistledown. I have often thought that if a man could build a large
cross, perhaps a score of paces from end to end, with arms
shaped just so – and if he could devise some means for making it
spin rapidly – why then he could fly like an eagle, soar above all
the lands and peoples of this earth."

Dardash paused and eyed the king, choosing his exact
moment. "Of course, such a contrivance is impossible."

Marcurades' face was rapt, glowing. "I disagree, Dardash – I
think one could be constructed."

"But the weight of the arms . . . ."

"It would be folly to use solid wood for that purpose,"
Marcurades cut in, his voice growing more fervent. "No, I see
light frameworks covered with wooden veneers, or skins, or –
better still – silk. Yes, *silk!*"

Dardash shook his head. "No man, not even the mightiest wrestler, could spin the arms fast enough."

"Like all stargazers, you are lacking in knowledge of what can be done with earthly substances like copper and water . . . and fire," Marcurades replied, beginning to pace in circles. "I can produce the power of ten men, of a *horse*, within a small compass. The main problem is to make that power subservient to my wishes. It has to be channelled, and . . . and . . ." Marcurades raised one finger, traced an invisible line vertically and then, his eyes abstracted disks of white light, began to move his hand in horizontal circles.

"From *this* . . . to *this*," he murmured, communing with himself. "There must be a way."

"I don't understand, sire," Dardash said, disguising the exultation that pounded within him. "What are you . . . ?"

"You'll see, stargazer." Marcurades turned back to the palace. "I think I'm going to surprise you."

"And I think I'm going to surprise *you*," Dardash said under his breath as he watched Marcurades stride away. Well satisfied with his morning's work, Dardash glanced at Nirrineen and felt a flicker of cold displeasure as he saw she was gazing at the figure of the departing king with a peculiar intensity.

The sooner my task here is complete, he thought irritably, *the better I'll like it*.

Urtarra's private apartment was a lavishly appointed room, the walls of which were hung with deep blue tapestries embroidered with astrological emblems. He had apologised to Dardash for the ostentation of its furnishings and trappings, explaining that as he was not truly an astrologer it was necessary for him to put on a bold and convincing show for the benefit of all other residents at the palace. Now he was squatting comfortably on his bed, looking much as he had done the first time Dardash had seen him – plump, oily, deceptively soft.

"I suppose I must congratulate you," he said reflectively. "Going aloft in a flying machine is one of the most dangerous things imaginable, and if you bring about the king's death without the use of magic your triumph has to be considered all the greater. I won't withhold your reward."

"Don't even think of trying," Dardash advised. "Besides, you have missed the whole point of my discourse – I *will* have to use magic. A great deal of magic."

"But if it is simply a matter of waiting until Marcurades and his machine fall from the sky, I don't see . . ."

"What you don't see is that the machine will not be capable of leaving the ground," Dardash interrupted, amazed that a man of Urtarra's experience could display such naïvety about the natural world. "Not without my assistance, anyway. Man, like all other animals, belongs to the ground, and there is no contrivance – no ingenious combination of levers and springs and feathers – which can raise him out of his natural element.

"Note that I said *natural* element, because it is the essence of magic that it defies nature. I intend to cast a spell over whatever machine Marcurades builds, and with the power of my magic that machine will bear him upwards, higher and higher into the realm of the gods, and then – when I judge the moment aright – the gods will become angry at the invasion of their domain by a mere mortal, and . . ."

"And you'll cancel your spell!" Urtarra clapped his hands to his temples. "It's perfect!"

Dardash nodded. "All of Bhitsala will see their king up there in the sky, far beyond the reach of ordinary men, and when he falls to his death – who but the gods could be responsible? Even Marcurades cannot aspire to the status of a deity and hope to go unpunished."

"I bow to you, Dardash," Urtarra said. "You have earned my undying gratitude."

"Keep it," Dardash said coldly. "I'm doing a specified job for a specified fee – and there is no more to it than that."

The days that followed required him to make a number of carefully-weighed decisions. On the one hand, he did not want to spend much time in the palace workshops for fear of becoming associated with the flying machine in people's minds, and thus attracting some blame for the final disaster; on the other hand, he needed to see what was happening so that he could work the appropriate magic. There was a plentiful supply of mana in the vicinity of Bhitsala – he could sense it in his enhanced youthfulness and vigour – but he had no wish to waste it with an illconceived spell. If mana was again returning to the world at large, perhaps sifting down from the stars, it behoved him to conserve it, especially as he aspired to live as a magician for a very long time, perhaps forever.

He was intrigued to see that Marcurades had divided the work of building his flying machine into two entirely separate parts. One team of carpenters was concerned with fashioning four wings of the lightest possible construction. The frameworks over which silk was to be stretched were so flimsy that strong cords had been used instead of wood in places where the members they joined always tended to move apart. Nevertheless, Dardash noted, the resulting structures were surprisingly stiff and his respect for Marcurades' capabilities increased, although he knew that all the work of the artisans was futile.

The king had exercised even more ingenuity in the device which was intended to spin the wings. At its heart was a large, well-reinforced copper container beneath which was a miniature furnace. The latter incorporated a bellows and was fired by coals and pitch. The invisible force which springs from boiling water travelled vertically upwards through a rigid pipe at the top of which was a slip ring. Four lesser pipes, all bent in the same direction, projected horizontally from the ring in the form of a swastika. When the furnace was lit the steam expelled from the end of the pipes caused the swastika to rotate at a considerable speed, and by decreasing pressure losses and improving lubrication and balance Marcurades was making it go faster every day.

Dardash watched the work without comment. He knew from his reading, and a certain amount of experimentation, that all should come to naught when the wings were attached to the pipes of the swastika. For no reason he could explain, the faster that wing-shaped objects travelled the more difficult they became to urge forward, and the resistance increased much more rapidly than one would have expected. Under normal conditions Marcurades' machine would have been able to produce no more than a feeble and faltering rotation of the wings, far short of the speed needed to create the inexplicable lightness required for flight, but the circumstances were far from normal.

Dardash prepared a simple kinetic sorcery and directed its power into the four newly-completed wings, altering their unseen physical nature in such a way that the faster they moved the *less* effort it took to increase their speed even further. He prudently remained in a distant part of the palace when Marcurades assembled his machine for the first time, but he knew precisely when the first test was carried out. An ornate ring he wore on his left hand began to vibrate slightly, letting him know that a certain amount of mana was being used up – the wings of the flying machine were spinning in a satisfactory manner.

Dardash visualised the hissing contraption beginning to stir and shiver, to exhibit the desire to leave the ground, and he strained his ears for evidence of one possible consequence. He knew that the king was reckless when in the grip of an enthusiasm, and if he were foolhardy enough to go aloft in the machine in its present form he would almost certainly be killed, and Dardash would be able to claim his reward earlier than planned. There came no cries of alarm, however, and he deduced that Marcurades had foreseen the need to control the machine once it soared up from the still air of the courtyard and into the turbulent breezes that forever danced above the cliffs.

I can wait, he thought, nodding his appreciation of the young king's engineering talent. *What are a few more days when measured against eternity*?

The news that the king had constructed a machine with which he intended to fly into the heavens spread through Bhitsala and the surrounding regions of Koldana in a very short time. There was to be no public ceremony connected with the first flight – indeed Marcurades was too engrossed in his new activity even to be aware of his subjects' feverish interest in it – but as stories spread further and became more lurid there was a general drift of population towards Bhitsala.

The city filled with travellers who had come to see the ruler borne aloft on the back of a mechanical dragon, eagle or bat, depending on which variation of the rumour they had encountered. Bhitsala's lodging houses and taverns experienced a profitable upsurge of trade and the atmosphere of excitement and celebration intensified daily, with runners coming down from the palace at frequent intervals to barter the latest scraps of information. People going about their routine business kept glancing up towards the white-columned royal residence, and such was the pitch of expectancy that every time a flock of seabirds rose from the cliffs an audible ripple of near-hysteria sped through the streets.

Dardash, while keeping himself closely informed of Marcurades' progress, made a show of being disinterested almost to the point of aloofness. He spent much of his time on the balcony of Urtarra's apartment, ostensibly engaged in astrological work, but in fact keeping watch on the western ramparts of the palace, behind which the flying machine was receiving finishing touches. During this period of idleness and waiting he would have appreciated the company of Nirrineen, but she had taken to associating a great deal with certain of the courtesans who attended the king. Urtarra had expressed the opinion that her absence was all to the good, as it meant she had less chance to become an embarrassment and Dardash had voiced his agreement. But he waxed more moody and surly, and ever more impatient, and as he scanned the foreshortened silhouette of the palace his eyes seemed, occasionally, to betray his true age.

"And not before time," was his sole comment when Urtarra arrived one day, in the trembling purple heat of noon, with the intelligence that Marcurades was on the point of making a trial flight. Dardash had already known that a significant event was about to occur, because the sensor ring on his left hand had been vibrating strongly for some time – evidence that the machine's wings were rotating at speed. He had also seen and heard the growing excitement in the city below. The population of Bhitsala appeared to have migrated like so many birds to rooftops and high window ledges, any place from which they could get a good view of the forthcoming miracle.

"This is a wonderful thing you are doing for the people of Koldana," Urtarra said as they stood together on the balcony, with the blue curvatures of the bay stretching away beneath them. His voice was low and earnest, as though he had begun to suffer last-minute doubts and was trying to drive them away.

"Just have my payment ready," Dardash said, giving him a disdainful glance.

"You have no need to worry on that . . ." Urtarra's speech faltered as the air was disturbed by a strange sound, a powerful and sustained fluttering which seemed to resonate inside the chest.

A moment later the king's flying machine lifted itself into view above the palace's western extremity.

The four rotating wings were visible as a blurry white disk, edged with gold, and slung beneath them was a gondola-shaped basket in which could be seen the figure of the king. Dardash's keen eyesight picked out weights suspended on ropes beneath the basket, giving the whole assemblage the same kind of stability as a pendulum, and it seemed to him that Marcurades had also added extra fitments at the top of the pipe which carried steam to the wing impellers.

A sigh of mingled wonder and adoration rose up from the watching throngs as the machine continued its miraculous ascent into the clear blue dome of the sky. At a dizzy height above the palace, almost at the limit of Dardash's vision, the king reached upwards to operate a lever, the insubstantial disk of the wings tilted slightly, and the machine swooped out over the line of the cliffs, out over the waters of the bay.

Ecstatic cheering, great slow-pulsing billows of sound, surged back and forth like tidal currents as Marcurades – godlike in his new power – steered his machine into a series of wide sweeps far above the wave crests.

"Now," Urtarra urged. "The time is *now*!"

"So be it," Dardash said, fingering the scrap of parchment on which the spell for the kinetic sorcery was written. He uttered a single polysyllabic word and tore the parchment in two.

At that instant the sun-gleaming shape of the flying machine was checked in its course, as though it had encountered an invisible obstacle. It wavered, faltered, then began to fall.

The sound that went up from the watching multitude was a vast wordless moan of consternation and shocked disbelief. Dardash listened to it for a moment, his face impassive, and was turning away from the balcony when two things happened to petrify him in mid-stride.

Far out across the water Marcurades' flying machine, which had been tilting over as it fell, abruptly righted itself and began to hover, neither losing nor gaining height. Simultaneously, a fierce pain lanced through Dardash's left hand. He snatched the sensor ring off his finger and threw it to the floor, where it promptly became white hot. Outside was a pounding silence as every one of Marcurades' subjects, not daring to breathe, prayed for his safety.

"The king flies," Urtarra said in a hushed voice. "He built better than you knew."

"I don't think so," Dardash said grimly. "Look! The machine's wings are scarcely turning. It should be falling!"

He strode to a chest where he had stored some of his equipment and returned with a silver hoop which he held out at arm's length. Viewed through the metal circle the hovering aircraft was a blinding, sun-like source of radiance. Dardash felt the beginnings of a terrible fear.

"What does it mean?" Urtarra said. "I don't . . ."

"That light is mana – the raw power behind magic." Dardash's throat had gone dry, thickening and deadening his voice. "Fantastic amounts of it are being expended to keep Marcurades and his machine aloft. I've never seen such a concentration."

"Does that mean there's another magician at work?"

"I wish that were all it meant," Dardash said. He lowered the silver hoop and stared at the flickering mote which was the flying machine. It had begun to move again, slowly losing height and drifting in towards the shore, and Dardash knew with bleak certainty that aboard it was a new kind of man – one who could use mana instinctively, in tremendous quantities, to satisfy his own needs and achieve his ambitions. Marcurades could tap and squander mana resources without even being aware of what he was doing, and Dardash now fully understood why the future divined for the king had been so cataclysmic. Such power, without the discipline and self-knowledge of the traditional sorcerers, could only corrupt. The mana-assisted achievement of each ambition would inspire others, each grander and more vainglorious than the one before, and the inevitable outcome would be evil and madness.

Dardash, all too conscious of the dangerous nature of the energy behind his profession, suddenly foresaw the rise of a new kind of tyrant – the spawning of monsters so corrupted by success and ambition, believing *themselves* to be the fountainheads of power, that they would eventually seek to dominate the entire world, and even be prepared to see it go up in flames if their desires were thwarted.

"I forbid it," he whispered, his fear giving way to resentment and a deep implacable hatred. "I, Dardash, say – *NO*!"

He ran back to the chest, driven by the knowledge that with each passing second Marcurades was a little closer to safety, and took from it a slim black rod. The wand had no power in itself, but it served to direct and concentrate magical energies. There was an unexpected noise in the next room and, glancing through the partially open door, Dardash saw Nirrineen coming towards him. Her expression was one of childish delight and her hands were at her throat, caressing a gold necklace.

"Look what the king has given me," she said, "Isn't it the most . . ."

"Stay out of here," Dardash shouted, trying to control his panic as he realised there was almost no time left in which to accomplish his purpose. He wheeled to face the balcony and the bright scene beyond it, pointed the wand and uttered a spell he had hoped never to use, a personal sacrilege, a destructive formula which used mana to combat and neutralise mana.

The flying machine disintegrated.

Its four wings flailed and fluttered off in different directions, and from the centre of the destruction the body of the machine plunged downwards like a mass of lead. There was a sputtering explosion as it struck the water, then it was gone, and Marcurades was lost, and all that remained of the young king and all his ambitions were spreading ripples of water and the four slow-tumbling wings which had borne him to his death. A lone sea bird shrieked in the pervading silence.

Dardash had time for one pang of triumph, then his vision dimmed and blurred. He looked at his hands and saw that they had withered into the semblance of claws, blotched and feeble, and he understood at once that his brief battle with Marcurades had been even more destructive than he had anticipated. In that one instant of conflict every trace of mana in the entire region had been annihilated, and he – Dardash – no longer had access to the magical power which had preserved his body.

"Murderer!" Nirrineen's voice seemed to reach him from another time, another existence. "You murdered the king!"

Dardash turned to face her. "You overestimate my powers, child," he soothed, motioning for Urtarra to move around behind her and block the exit. "What makes you think that a humble dabbler in simple magic could ever . . . ?"

He broke off as he saw Nirrineen's revulsion at his appearance, evidence that more than a century of hard living had taken a dreadful toll of his face and body. Evidence of his guilt.

Nirrineen shook her head, and with near-magical abruptness she was gone. Her fleeing footsteps sounded briefly and were lost in the mournful wailing that had begun to pervade the room from outside as the people of Bhitsala absorbed the realisation that their king was dead.

"You should have stopped her," Dardash said to Urtarra, too weak and tired to sound more than gently reproachful. "She has gone to fetch the palace guard, and now neither of us will ever . . ."

He stopped speaking as he saw that Urtarra had sunk down on a couch, hands pressed to his temples, eyes dilated with a strange horror, seeing but not seeing.

"So it has finally happened to you, soothsayer – now you can foresee your own death." Dardash spoke with intuitive understanding of what was happening in Urtarra's mind. "But do not waste what little time remains to you. Let me know that my sacrifice has not been in vain, that the whore wasn't carrying Marcurades' seed. Give me proof that no other mana-monsters will arise to usurp magicians and wreak their blind and ignorant havoc on the world."

Urtarra appeared deaf to his words, but he raised one hand and pointed at the opposite wall of the room. The blue tapestries acquired a tremulous depth they had not previously possessed, came alive with images of times yet to be. The images changed rapidly, showing different places and different eras, but they had some elements in common.

Always there was fire, always thee was destruction, always there was death on a scale that Dardash had never conceived.

And against these fearful backgrounds there came a procession of charismatic, mana-rich figures. Knowledge, foreknowledge, was again vouchsafed to Dardash in wordless whispers, and unfamiliar names reverberated within his head . . .

Alexander . . . Julius Caesar . . . Tamburlaine . . .

The sky grew dark with the shadow of thousands of wings, annihilation rained from great airborne ships, creating a lurid backdrop for the strutting figure of Adolf Hitler . . .

Dardash covered his eyes with his hands and sank to a kneeling position, and remained that way without moving until the sound of heavy footsteps and the clatter of armour told him the palace guards had arrived. And the stroke of the sword, not long delayed, came like a kindly friend, bringing the only reward for which he retained any craving.

All Orbit Books are available at your bookshop or newsagent, or can be ordered from the following address:
Futura Books,
Cash Sales Department,
P.O. Box 11,
Falmouth,
Cornwall TR10 9EN.

Alternatively you may fax your order to the above address. Fax No. 0326 76423.

Payments can be made as follows: Cheque, postal order (payable to Macdonald & Co (Publishers) Ltd) or by credit cards, Visa/Access. Do not send cash or currency. UK customers: please send a cheque or postal order (no currency) and allow 80p for postage and packing for the first book plus 20p for each additional book up to a maximum charge of £2.00.

B.F.P.O. customers please allow 80p for the first book plus 20p for each additional book.

Overseas customers including Ireland, please allow £1.50 for postage and packing for the first book, £1.00 for the second book, and 30p for each additional book.

NAME (Block Letters) ....

ADDRESS ....

....

☐ I enclose my remittance for _____

☐ I wish to pay by Access/Visa Card

Number ☐☐☐☐☐☐☐☐☐☐☐☐☐☐☐☐☐

Card Expiry Date ☐☐☐☐